A Modern Life

Jane Turley

Sweet and Salty Books

Sweet and Salty Books
www.sweetandsaltybooks.net

A catalogue record of this book is available from the British Library.

ISBN 978-0-9928754-3-5

Cover by Design for Writers
Formatting by Polgarus Studio
www.polgarusstudio.com

Also by Jane Turley

The
Changing
Room
A British Comedy of Love, Loss and Laughter
www.changingroomnovel.net

Discover more of Jane's writing on her blog, The Witty
Ways of a Wayward Wife at www.janeturley.net. Connect
with her via Facebook at
www.facebook.com/janeturleywriter
or on Twitter @turleytalks

Author's Note

This collection of stories is a reflection, not only of my imagination, but of all my emotions, experiences, interests and beliefs as well as all that I see happening in this modern life, both good and bad. That is why, as you will discover, it encompasses many themes and genres: from gay marriage and office banter to serious drama and slapstick comedy. To give you the opportunity to discover these according to your taste and mood I have classified them as "sweet" for the lighter stories, "salty" for the serious ones and "sweet and salty" for those with a mixture of humour and pathos. I do hope you find something you enjoy.

Contents

Sweet

Pork Chops and Promiscuity

Judith was a lesbian. Only she didn't have short hair and she didn't wear wooden beads. Neither did she have a girlfriend with a moustache and legs like a Russian shotputter. In fact, Judith didn't have a girlfriend at all; she preferred the anonymity of one-night stands with girls picked up in gay bars and communal changing rooms. Judith particularly liked the changing rooms at the exclusive gym she attended where all the tanned PR girls hung-out, stripped to the waist, chatting nonsensically about their executive boyfriends and the latest skincare products. Whilst the nubile objects of Judith's affection compared the benefits of the latest three-for-the-price-of-two offers in Boots with make-up bags gifted with a purchase of two face creams in Debenhams, Judith would happily eye-up their scantily covered buttocks.

Judith's own choice of underwear was hipsters, as they flattered her slender hips but, as a voyeur, she preferred thongs. Often she would imagine ripping them off with her teeth and, after rampant sex, flossing with them in the same way she might do after enjoying a particularly good pork chop. Not that Judith should eat pork because it was against her religion. Well, her father's religion. Anyway, it didn't really matter about Judith's fondness for pork chops anymore as her father had disowned her when she'd told him that she was "coming out" and that she'd rather die than spend another evening, at his behest, with his best friend's son who had a PhD in engineering. That last dismal night with Englebert had resulted in a massive showdown - the culmination of years of Judith's self-hate for being her father's lackey. The acne-covered Englebert would have tested even the most stalwart socialite but, since Judith found nothing remotely interesting about the internal workings of office photocopiers, and had no knowledge of the functionalities of dynamic equilibrium, the evening had held even less interest than her great aunt's funeral. And Aunt Florrie had been a hundred and six when she died and only two people under the age of ninety, excluding Judith and her parents, had turned up. So it had been exceptionally dull.

Of course, there were good things and bad things about not having your father's love. Or his money. In fact, Judith's life had been somewhat difficult for six months when, without the comfort of her father's allowance, Judith had been forced to wait tables, in addition to her office job, to pay her bills. Although Judith enjoyed prying on her customers' conversations and flirting with city workers in order to elicit a big tip, it had been an enormous relief when her father was run over by the no 33 bus. In his statement, the driver had declared he hadn't seen Mr Freud crossing the road; a fact which Judith thought highly unlikely as her father weighed twenty stone and had been walking his Great Dane, Hildegard. However, it also seemed unlikely that the bus driver was an assassin and Judith wasn't one to complain about minor details. So, even though poor Hildegard had also perished, Judith was finally relinquished from her father's influence and took comfort in the knowledge that Hildegard's retinas were used to restore the sight of a Chihuahua from Golders Green.

Unlike Judith, her mother had been distraught at the news of the tragic accident. Indeed she'd been distraught until the day Solomon's will revealed that there was more than enough money for mother and daughter to live in luxury for the rest of their lives. Judith and her mother celebrated with champagne and pork medallions on a bed of exotic rice. Nevertheless, Judith's mother was a good woman and kept her joy well hidden, wearing black for six whole weeks and impressing all the neighbours with her solemnity. Until she met the new head butcher at Waitrose and was spotted barbecuing spare ribs and drinking sherry on the Sabbath.

So, it was shortly after her father's death, and her mother's exodus to Spain on a prolonged tour of the vineyards, that Judith found herself at a crossroads in life. Having temporarily handed over the management of her father's pawnbroking business to Jerri Scholar, her father's deputy, Judith continued with her office job whilst pondering her single status and the future of Solomon's

Gold Mines. Judith didn't trust Jerri Scholar because his name was, in fact, Gerry Schulberg and Judith had a deep-seated mistrust of people who changed their names for fashionable reasons. After all, this was the twenty-first century and none but the most bigoted was the least concerned by the fact that she was an (ex) Jewess with a penchant for young girls and pork chops. Not that Judith broadcasted her sexuality but, when she'd had fleeting affairs with younger women dissatisfied with their boyfriends, none of them seemed that bothered by either her sexuality or their own changing sexual preferences. Modern life was one big new adventure which, at times, young adults and teenagers seemed to consume faster than wholly appropriate - even to Judith, who was still only thirty-one.

However, Judith was not about to knock the society which, more or less, had accepted her ways. Particularly as she had recently discovered that, if she chose carefully, she could also solicit the attentions of older married women wishing to spice up their flagging sex lives and whose husbands thought female one-on-one titillating rather than grounds for divorce. As it turned out, Judith liked mature women as much as she liked younger women. Although younger women had the benefit of the freshness and enthusiasm of youth, the experience and determination of older women to obtain at least one more orgasm before they died impressed Judith, and more than made up for any sagging buttocks. Judith's only exception to this mantra was women who had sagging buttocks, breasts which touched their knees, and who also participated in aqua-aerobics. Having witnessed the carcass of an elderly aqua-aerobics swimmer hauled inelegantly from the pool one day, Judith had decided aqua-aerobics was a precursor to sudden death. The image of the bulging body, complete with yellow rubber cap and frilled costume, would remain imprinted on her memory forever.

So it was one day at work, whilst Judith was contemplating her future and refilling the photocopier (about which she now had more knowledge of its internal workings than what she felt wholly comfortable with) that the unexpected and yet, perhaps also the inevitable, happened. Out of her employer's office came a vision of loveliness so great that Judith's heart fluttered with the stirrings of lust and, very possibly, love. Judith had been wondering if love and marriage was something that happened only to heterosexuals. She had almost entirely resigned herself to a life of physically satisfying but emotionally barren intercourse when Shelley, eighteen-and-a-half with big brown eyes and hair from a L'Oreal advert, tripped gaily into the open-plan office with the aptly named Mr Hands following close behind, his palms hovering over her curvaceous derrière.

So the delightful Shelley joined the team at Handy Hands' Stationery Suppliers and became the object of both Judith and Mr Hands' desire. Unlike the salacious Mr Hands who could barely stop himself salivating over Shelley, Judith found herself adopting traits that she had previously thought more particular to love-struck heteros:

gazing into space, doodling hearts on her notebooks and maintaining a safe distance from her love interest in case of embarrassing rejection. As the weeks went by, Judith found it increasingly awkward when Shelley would pull up a chair, her soft breasts pouring over the top of her cheap low-cut tops, and ask Judith to demonstrate the finer details of Excel spreadsheets. Unfortunately, Judith would often imagine herself sucking Shelley's sweet pink nipples and was unable to concentrate on the job in hand which, for the purposes of demonstrating Excel, was rather a hindrance.

So with love in her heart and confusion in her logic, Judith stayed on at Handy Hands' Stationery Suppliers despite the fact that she was sure Jerri/Gerry was on the fiddle. Profits at Solomon's Gold Mines were down and Jerri's excuses about the gold price crashing, whilst seemingly plausible, didn't tally with her examination of the spreadsheets. She supposed that Jerri thought that because she'd only worked in a small office and had never been ruthlessly ambitious he didn't think her capable of spotting any irregularities. However, the fact was that Judith had inherited more of her father's aptitude for numbers than her mother's aptitude for the consumption of Spanish Cava.

The unhealthy situation came to a head one day when Judith, stomach aching and with a splitting headache caused by her unrequited love, was not at her best. Feeling particularly irritated that she'd run out of staples just as she was about to affix her final spreadsheet of the day, she dutifully headed down to the stationery cupboard, deluxe stapler in hand, to replenish her supplies before packing up and returning to her flat to spend the evening leaving woeful messages on Facebook. Judith was in two minds about Facebook as occasionally her exes would leave encouraging comments about her now undesired single status but, for the most part, Judith was besieged with a stream of photographs of lattes or cream cakes. These visual feasts only served to make her more depressed as, although Judith didn't have a weight problem, she didn't need to be reminded that some women could eat anything they wanted and still not have to work-out. So, feeling somewhat peeved about her situation in life, Judith refilled her stapler and pocketed the remainder of the packet. She was returning down the corridor, wondering if the news about her stapler being refilled would be sufficiently interesting to post on Facebook, when a loud squeal reverberated from the broom cupboard. Judith realised the squeal was that of a woman in distress and, more importantly, a woman whose high-pitched girly squeal was instantly recognisable as that of her beloved Shelley.

With her adrenaline running high, Judith threw open the door to the broom cupboard aghast at the thought of Shelley clinging to a top shelf, the portable steps having fallen away. But what Judith found was not Shelley holding on for dear life and about to fall into her arms but the poor girl wedged up against a stack of disinfectant, cleaning cloth in hand, wearing an expression of sheer terror. In front of the terrified Shelley, with his head buried in her breasts and a hand up her skirt, was Mr Hands grunting and moaning like a sow in labour.

As Judith absorbed the ghastly scene, her gaze locked with Shelley's pleading eyes. "Help me," mouthed Shelley as Mr Hands' fingers encroached inside her knickers. Shelley's pitiful appeal pierced Judith's heart and reservations, and with explosive fury Judith marched into the broom cupboard, grabbed Mr Hands' testicles as if she was going to bite into a massive pork chop and stapled them with all her might. Mr Hands screamed. And screamed. And with a final scream of ear-piercing stupendousness, Mr Hands collapsed to the floor writhing in agony, tears flooding down his beetroot face.

"You bastard," said Judith and, as she was never one to do anything by halves, bent down and stapled his testicles, not once, but twice more to be absolutely certain Mr Hands would never, ever, touch her dear Shelley again.

On completing her rescue mission, Judith held out her hand to the trembling Shelley and the two of them retreated to the office, cleared their desks, deleted all the electronic spreadsheets, shredded the paper ones, and sojourned to the Chinese restaurant for a dinner of sweet and sour pork balls accompanied by Spanish Cava. It was over a second helping of the pork balls that Judith, her emotions still running high and slightly intoxicated by the wine, declared her undying love to Shelley.

Not knowing what to expect, Judith held her breath at the possibility that pork balls might be thrown in her face. So it was a huge relief and surprise for Judith, even bigger than when her father had been mowed down by the no 33, when the almost inconceivable happened: Shelley declared her undying love in return. It transpired that Shelley had loved Judith since the day she'd joined Handy Hands' Stationery Suppliers and the only reason why Shelley hadn't declared her love was that she had no idea that Judith was also a lesbian. In her innocence, Shelley had been led to believe that most lesbians had moustaches and legs like a Russian shot-putter and that Judith, who had neither a moustache nor unwholesome legs, could therefore not be a lesbian. As for herself, Shelley believed she was a misfortunate rare exception to the lesbian rule and, lacking interest in hairy ladies with muscular thighs, she would be doomed to a life without love.

So perhaps it goes without saying that Judith and Shelley got married and lived happily ever after. But in this case, not before Judith had first fired Jerri/Gerry for embezzlement and discovered her father's payments for a lease to a flat registered to a woman who, coincidentally, shared the same surname as the bus driver who had run over her father and poor Hildegard. On balance, Judith decided her mother didn't need to know this information as it was pointless spoiling her new-found happiness. As Judith deleted the evidence she surmised that, even though she was still in the learning phase of life, she'd already discovered that all over the world people were screwing each other and it didn't really matter what race, religion or sexuality you were. Neither did it matter whether you were fat or thin or beautiful or ugly. Or even if you did aqua-aerobics. All that mattered was that you got to share a little love.

Trouble in the Office

A loud screech reverberated around the office.

"Oh my God!" screamed Cheryl, jumping up from her desk, her chair falling over behind her.

"What is it?" sighed Steve, looking up from his PC where he'd been looking at Trish from Essex with bigger than average breasts.

"It's a mouse!"

"Is that all? I thought you'd stapled your fingers to the invoices," said Steve, bookmarking the dating site for further investigation.

"It's in my drawer!"

"Is that your drawer or your drawers?" said Steve, leaning back in his chair, hands clasped behind his head.

"Just get rid of it!"

"Yeah, do us a favour," yelled Adrian from across the office. "Any more of Cheryl's sagas and I'm gonna drown myself in the water butt."

"It's eating my rice cakes!"

Steve pushed his revolving chair back from his desk and slid over to Cheryl's desk like a professional ice skater.

"So what do I get as a reward if I get rid of it? A date?" said Steve, eyeing up Cheryl's bottom.

"Anything, anything! Just get rid of it or I'm going to faint."

"Right, a date it is," said Steve, winking at Adrian. What a beautiful set-up. For six months Steve had failed to date Cheryl and then, quite by chance, he discovered her phobia whilst they'd been having a cigarette by the bins and a mouse had scuttled passed. "Now where exactly is this mouse?"

"There," said Cheryl, pointing at the little grey mouse ferreting amongst her stationery and nibbling her rice cakes.

"What a lovely little fella," said Steve, picking up the mouse by the tail and dangling it in front of Cheryl's face.

"Stop it, stop it!"

"A date then?"

"Yes, yes!"

"Okay then." Steve cupped the mouse leaving a little gap between his fingers. A little soft face with brown eyes and long whiskers appeared. "He's a beauty."

"What are you going to do with it?" said Cheryl, throwing the rice cakes in the bin.

"Shred it," yelled Adrian.

"You can't do that!" said Cheryl. "It's a mouse."

"But you don't like mice. So what does it matter?" said Steve.

"That doesn't mean I want to kill it."

"Women. So bloody difficult. I'll take it outside and release it. Happy?"

"Yes. Here, take the rice cakes for it." Cheryl picked the rice cakes back out of the bin and popped them in Steve's jacket pocket. "He's probably hungry."

"You could put it on the factory floor. That'll close us down for a week," said Mike, sipping his lukewarm coffee and sauntering over from his desk by the photocopier. "I could do with a holiday."

"Good point," replied Steve. "I'd better get rid of it fast."

Steve cupped his hands tight again and threaded his way out the office, stopping to show the little furry creature to everyone and taking pleasure in the murmurs of appreciation. Just as he was trying to negotiate the door with his shoulder, it flew open and in hurried Rich, red faced and flustered, waving a box file in the air.

"What you got there, mate?" said Rich, avoiding a collision with Steve and eyeing up his cupped hands.

"A mouse."

"Christ. Get rid of it quick. That could shut us down for a week."

"I know, I know. Right then, mousey. Say goodbye to the pretty lady." Steve held up the mouse and squeaked, "Goodbye Cheryl, see you at Finnegan's on Friday."

The office rang out with laughter, even Cheryl giggled as she sat back down, picking up her invoices again.

"Hurry up, mate," said Rich. "I've got an important announcement."

Steve pushed past and hot-footed it towards the Gents at the end of the corridor.

"Ladies and gentlemen," boomed Rich. "I have announcement. I, Richie the Rich, smart-arse Wokingham, have won over the MD."

A whoop of delight and a round of applause rippled round the office.

"Hurrah," said Adrian, flicking a paperclip across the room.

"Jolly good show, old bean," said Darren, peering out from behind his spectacles whilst blowing up a battleship on his computer.

"Well, come on then. Tell us the astounding news, smart-arse," said Mike, throwing his coffee cup in Cheryl's bin and ambling back to his desk.

Rich opened up the box file and pulled out a pink cardboard box and held it up for display like a placard at a boxing match.

"Friends, Romans, plebs of the office, I, Richie the Rich, have today persuaded the managing director to change the Mrs Fanny's fairy cake packaging to…PINK."

An even bigger round of whooping and applause echoed around the office as Rich beamed and took a bow of thanks.

"And tell us, Rich," said Adrian as the cheering subsided, "What colour was it before?"

"Umm… it was…it was…red," said Rich, grimacing to the sound of a unanimous groan from his colleagues.

"Did you say 'red'?" said Mike, grabbing the box file and pulling out an almost identical pink box. "So, you've got the box changed from this 'red'…or should I say this 'dark shade of pink' to a 'lighter shade of pink.' Is that right?" Mike patted Rich on the back as Rich's expression turned from elation to despair. "Well done, mate. There's an award waiting for you."

Rich sat down at the nearest empty desk, clasping his head in his hands. "God, I hate this job. Product development, my arse. My whole life wasted on cake packaging."

"Cheer up," said Adrian. "Remember your success with the flapjack? Sales went up twenty percent in one week when you changed the packaging from black to white."

"And the italics on the chocolate chip cookies looked classy. My mum said so," said Cheryl, looking up from her paperwork with a sympathetic smile.

Rich banged his head up and down on the desk in frustration. "I hate cakes. I hate cakes. I HATE cakes."

The office door burst open again and Steve rushed back in. "You'll never guess what I've just seen." Everyone stopped laughing at Rich and looked at Steve with anticipation. "It's the biggest floater I've ever seen. In the Gents. It's massive!"

"I gotta see this," said Adrian.

"Me too," said Mike.

"Come on, come and have a look!" Steve glanced at Rich still sprawled over the desk. "And you too, mate. Looks like you've had another glorious success."

"Oh, if I must," said Rich, jumping up, revitalised by the thought of the world's largest floater being discovered at Mrs Fanny's cake factory.

"Unbelievable," said Cheryl as the men rushed out of the office and down the corridor chatting and laughing.

"Fifteen grown men going to admire a floater," said Babs, pulling out her nail file from her top drawer. "If only they worked as hard at work as they do at being idiots we'd double our output and get a bonus."

"No chance," said Maureen, glancing up from her keyboard and pushing her glasses back up her nose. "I've been here twenty-five years and there's not a day goes by without talk of flatulence or women. I don't know how I've put up with it."

"How do you think that mouse got in your desk, Cheryl?" said Babs.

"I've no idea."

"Do you think somebody put it there?"

"Why would they?"

"Because of your phobia."

"Nobody knows about it."

"Except Steve. Remember that day we saw the mouse by the bins?"

"Oh, it'll definitely be that Steve," said Maureen, interrupting. "He's got the eyes for you, Cheryl. Any excuse to talk to you and he's there. Now he's got a date out of you."

"I thought you fancied him. Why haven't you gone out with him yet?" said Babs.

"I've seen him looking at women's pictures on the net," said Cheryl, despondently.

"That's just men's stuff," said Maureen. "Doesn't mean a thing."

"Let's have a look at his PC," giggled Babs.

"Why not?" said Maureen, heaving her buxom frame out of her chair and bustling over to Steve's desk. "Let's see what the naughty fellow has been up to."

Babs and Cheryl got up from their desks and peered over Maureen's shoulder.

"We shouldn't really be doing this," said Cheryl.

"Oh, stuff and nonsense," said Maureen, tapping away on Steve's keyboard. "Right, what's he got in his bookmarks? Hmm…Trish from Essex…Sharon from Doncaster…Kylie from London."

"See, I told you. How could I date a bloke like that?" said Cheryl as Maureen flicked through pages of dating sites featuring big-busted blondes.

"What a perv. Let's see what he's got in his pictures," said Babs.

Maureen clicked open Steve's pictures. The three women looked at the one picture and then at each other in amazement.

"It's me," said Cheryl, "at last year's Christmas party."

"Blimey, he must be smitten. He's even painted a love heart in the corner," said Babs in awe.

"Take it from me," said Maureen. "I've got five sons. These other girls are just fantasy stuff. It's you he wants."

"Do you think so?" said Cheryl.

"Definitely. Now back to work, girls," said Maureen as footsteps and laughter reverberated down the corridor again. "I hear the motley crew returning."

"Ladies, ladies, ladies. What do I have for you?" said Rich, entering the office just as the women were getting seated. "Only the world's largest floater." Rich held up his phone for everyone to see. "Yes, captured on film for all eternity - the world's one and only, supersized, cake-induced floater!"

"You're disgusting," said Babs, wrinkling her nose at the distant sight of the floater. "I don't want to see it."

"Me neither," said Maureen. "I've seen enough number twos in my time. The plumber practically lives at my house."

Rich rushed over to Cheryl's desk. "What about you, Cheryl? Isn't it a beauty?"

"That's revolting," said Cheryl, grimacing at the close-up on Rich's phone.

"It's champion," said Rich. "What d'you reckon, Steve?"

"Quality, quality," said Steve. "Any man would be proud of that."

"No one's admitting to it though," said Rich. "What a spoil sport. And it's an historic floater."

"I reckon it's the MD's. I always said he was a big turd," said Steve.

"How right you are," said Rich, grinning. "And now, the only thing left to do is…to email it to all the company!"

Rich and Steve huddled over Rich's PC, chuckling as they downloaded the photo.

"Hmm…there's something missing," said Steve, standing back to admire the picture from another angle. "Paint some candles on it."

"I'll put a frill around it as well. And a ribbon at the front," said Rich with the enthusiasm of a schoolboy.

"And put a couple of Smarties either side of the candles," said Steve.

"Perfect," said Rich, admiring their handiwork. "And now to send it."

"I've got it!" cried Darren.

"Crikey, that was quick," said Rich. "My email's slow today."

"Not the floater, Rich. The Class A Russian spy sub. Finally found the little fucker. Blown it to smithereens."

"Good job, Darren. Now find my desk will you? I haven't seen it under all this shite for a week," said Rich, chuckling at his own repartee.

"Hey, Steve," said Cheryl, leaning towards Steve who was now back at his desk. "Thanks again for getting rid of the mouse. It was alright, wasn't it?"

"Yes, it was fine."

"I was just wondering…well, I'm free tonight. If you wanted to bring that date forward?"

"Really?"

"Yes."

"Well, okay," said Steve. "That would be…fantas…nice."

Steve and Cheryl broke off their conversation as Mike ran into the office brushing cigarette ash off his jacket. "Mr Johnson's coming!" he shouted.

"Quick, everyone. Back to work," cried Rich. "The Führer is on his way."

A deathly hush crept over the room as the door opened and in marched Mr Johnson, the managing director.

"Who sent this out?" demanded Mr Johnson, waving a picture of the floater. Reluctantly, Rich and Steve raised their hands whilst their colleagues smirked. "Wokingham? I might have known it would be you. And you too Smith? Get down to my office. Both of you. We need to talk."

Rich and Steve rose from their chairs and with hunched shoulders followed Mr Johnson out of the office, a host of whispers and giggles bursting out behind them. They walked in silence, giving each other miserable glances, until they were standing before the managing director's desk.

"Before we get down to business," said Mr Johnson, making himself comfortable in his plush chair. "Do either of you know about that caged mouse in the Gents? It could put us out of business for a week."

"Um…it's mine, sir," said Steve.

"For heaven's sake, Smith. What were you thinking of?"

"Just a scheme to get Cheryl on a date, sir."

"Christ, you're not still trying to get your leg over? Well, I've got to admire your inventiveness. Next time avoid mice though, will you? I've got a business to run."

"Yes, sir," replied Steve, standing to attention.

"Now about this cake," said Mr Johnson, picking up his printed email.

"Cake?" replied Rich. "What cake?"

"The chocolate log, Wokingham. It's a brilliant idea. Why didn't you tell me this morning, when you were here with the packaging?"

"Um…I…we were still working on it," said Rich, searching for an excuse.

"We wanted to canvas opinions, sir," said Steve, coming to the rescue. "With the email."

"Well, it's brilliant," said Mr Johnson, beaming profusely. "I don't know why I didn't think of it before. "Mrs Fanny's Birthday Chocolate Log." It'll sell millions. Put it into production immediately!"

Steve and Rich glanced at each other and grinned; perhaps Mr Johnson wasn't such a big turd after all.

Caught Short

Terri's bike wobbled as the Lamborghini whipped past her doing about sixty mph, sucking the breath out of her and almost making her career into Lisa on her inside.

"Stupid idiot!" yelled Lisa as the slick silver car flew past. The swarthy male driver, eyes shielded by dark sunglasses, made not even the slightest indication of seeing the two shaken cyclists.

"Twat," said Terri, regaining her breath and pulling a strand of her long black hair that had escaped from underneath her helmet from her mouth. "What a jerk driving at that speed down a country lane. He could've killed us."

"I've scratched my arm on those thorn bushes," replied Lisa, gently rubbing her left arm which now bore a cluster of bright red grazes and a trace of blood. "We were lucky though. It could've been worse."

"Maybe he'll plough himself into a lamp post and do the world a service by making one less moron with a flash car on the planet," continued Terri, watching the sleek form disappear, tail lights flashing and tyres screeching as the driver negotiated a tight bend. "Let's stop at that lay-by ahead and have a drink. I could do with a breather after that fright."

"Okay, I'll race you," Lisa replied, pushing down hard on her pedals, her tanned legs and arms taut as she raced away. "I'm gonna beat you!" she screamed as she took the corner.

Terri's legs pumped furiously up and down, her knuckles white and her hair flying loose again as she closed the gap.

"Hey, the Lamborghini," panted Lisa, slowing down as Terri caught up with her.

The car was pulled up in the lay-by a short distance ahead with the driver's door wide open and the radio blasting out disco music into the quiet countryside.

"Let's see what's up," said Terri. "Maybe we'll have the chance to get our own back."

The girls raced up to the car and dismounted. Taking a good look around and peering into the car, they couldn't see any signs of the reckless, speeding owner.

"Wow, look at that interior!" said Lisa, pulling off her helmet to reveal her blonde bob and pixie face. She slipped into the smooth leather seat and ran her fingers lovingly around the steering wheel. "Just imagine having enough cash to buy one of these."

"Yeah, that guy must be loaded. Pity he's such a clown, otherwise it might have been worth making a move on him. But I think we should give him a lesson instead," giggled Terri with delight. "Do you see what I see?"

"Oh you mean these?" Lisa pulled the keys from the ignition. "And what about this?" Lisa picked the mobile phone off the passenger seat and tossed it out to Terri with the keys. "How careless leaving a car like this open. He must be totally arrogant or so rich he doesn't give a damn if anyone nicks it. Where do you think he's gone?"

"I don't know. But hardly anyone comes this way. Maybe he was caught short and thought it was safe to leave the car for a moment," replied Terri, jangling the keys with a wicked smile. "I've got a plan; let's hide further up the road before he comes back."

Positioning themselves at a safe distance, the girls soon spotted a leg appearing over the stile in the lay-by followed by the body of a tall athletic man in his late thirties with film star looks.

"He's a dish," whispered Lisa.

"He sure is. All the more reason to make him suffer," said Terri, perusing the jean clad demi-god. "And I know just how to do it."

The man climbed back into the driver's seat, pulling the door shut behind him. After a brief moment he began to search his pockets. Then his head disappeared down into the footwell and then over to the passenger seat. Finally, he got out of the car and started to retrace his footsteps towards the stile.

"COO…EEE!" Terri held the keys high in the air and waved them to and fro like a tempting treat for a puppy. "Were you looking for these?"

The man swivelled around towards the girls, and removed his glasses, assessing the situation, and the girls' clinging attire.

"And maybe this?" said Lisa, tossing the phone high in the air, catching it and sticking it down the inside of her bra as the man looked on with interest.

"Geez, he's seriously hot," said Terri, speaking through gritted teeth as she dangled the keys. "I'm just gonna love this."

"I see you ladies have me compromised," said the man with a slight twitch of his mouth.

"You could've killed us back there," said Lisa.

"I'm sorry. I'm on my way to a meeting and took a wrong turn. I'm running late."

"That's not a proper apology. Just excuses," said Terri.

"Sorry again. Now can I have my keys back now you've had your fun?" said the man. "I need to go."

"He's a pretty cool dude," said Lisa. "He doesn't look in the least perturbed. If anything he's amused."

"I'm afraid you're going to have to work for your keys. Let me see…twenty press-ups should do it," said Terri.

"Are you serious?" replied the man.

"Yep," said Terri, trying to keep a straight face.

"And then I can have my keys and phone?"

"Maybe."

"Jesus. Women." The man sighed, squatted down on the floor and quickly did twenty press-ups with a practised efficiency. Then he sprang upright and held out his palm. "Right, job done. Hand them over."

"I'm not sure if that was good enough," said Terri, turning to Lisa. "What do you think? Shall we give them to him? I think he needs to work harder."

"It's very hot today though. Maybe he needs to cool down first?" said Lisa, suggestively.

"Hmm…I believe you're right," said Terri, turning back to the handsome stranger. "Okay, Mr Speedy, strip off."

"For God's sake, what are you girls playing at?" said the man with exasperation. "Just give me my keys back before I lose my patience."

"Oooh, you're soooo gorgeous when you're angry," said Terri, revelling in the man's annoyance. "Now do you want your keys back or not? It's a long way home."

"I don't believe this," said the man, his impatience soon replaced by tacit compliance as the clinking of the keys caught his attention again. "But you'd better give me my keys back this time, or I won't be responsible for my actions."

"It's a deal," said Terri, grinning.

Looking uncomfortable, the stranger undid the buttons on his shirt, revealing a muscular torso, and placed it neatly on the bonnet of the car. Terri waved the keys once more as his fingers fumbled over the buckle on his belt.

"Yes, and the trousers," said Terri, unable to contain her laughter, "And don't forget the pants. You can leave the socks on though - I like a man in the buff with his socks on. It speaks so much of his style."

Lisa erupted with laughter.

"Bitch," said the man, pulling his off his jeans and flinging them into a nearby bush. Then with a dramatic flourish he whipped off his underpants and hurtled them across the car bonnet into the lay-by where they caught on a fence post, hanging in the air like a white flag of defeat.

"I hope you like what you see," said the man, his sarcasm turning to humour as the girls giggled out loud.

"He's a big boy," said Lisa.

"Yes, and if he gets any bigger I'll be able to hang my washing out," replied Terri, admiring the man's assets.

At that moment the high pitched voices of the Bee Gees and a disco classic reverberated from the car.

"Okay, pretty boy. Dance. Travolta style," said Terri, inspired by the thumping music.

"You've got to be kidding me," said the man, raising his eyes to the heavens in bewilderment.

"Nope. Dance. Come on, get moving. We haven't got all day!"

The man stared at Terri's resolute face, and then reluctantly started to sway his hips while the sexy beat that had swept generations onto the dance floor blasted out into the countryside.

"I've seen more movement in a corpse," shouted Terri. "You can do better. No need to be shy!"

The man stared vehemently back at Terri, speeding up his gyrations as Terri continued heckling him.

"Come on, baby. Shake that booty. You know you want to!"

Lisa was bent double with laughter, tears running down her cheeks, as wearing only his socks, the man started exaggerating his hip movements to the chorus of Saturday Night Fever.

"Move those hips. Put some passion into it. Shake that butt!" said Terri.

The man turned around and wriggled his bottom furiously at the girls.

"That's more like it," cried Terri, enjoying her role. "Now the arm actions. Show us your groove!"

Up went the man's right arm pointing to the sky and then down to the opposite hip. Turning back around to face them, up went his left arm and back down to his right hip. Now completely uninhibited, the man performed to the girls like a disco king.

"Oh my God, I think I'm going to wet my knickers," said Lisa, now prostrate upon the floor, clutching her stomach and gasping for breath between bursts of uncontrollable giggles. "I think I'm gonna die and go to heaven."

"I'm already there," grinned Terri, casting her eyes over the stranger's naked body. Returning her grin, the man gyrated his pelvis for her appreciation. "Boy, he can really move."

"Oh my goodness, I think I'm going to pass out," said Lisa, wiping away her tears.

"Come on, it's the last chorus, give it your all. We want to see some real effort!" cried Terri.

The man continued dancing with abandon until the song came to an end. Terri held out the keys. Breathless and rosy cheeked, the stranger strode unashamedly over to the girls. Bending down, he retrieved his phone from Lisa's bra as she lay curled up in a ball in the middle of the road, still laughing.

"Naughty girl," said the man before turning to Terri and holding his hand out to receive the keys. "And you, young lady. I guess you'd like to see more of my moves?"

"I…um…ah…" Terri's eyes flicked downwards, her cheeks turning crimson. When she looked up the man was grinning with amusement. Terri dropped the keys in his palm.

"Hmm…lost for words," said the stranger. "That makes a change. Now unfortunately, I have a meeting to attend. A pity. I was just getting into the mood." The man's eyes twinkled with merriment. "But who knows, maybe we'll meet again."

Collecting his scattered clothes, the man put his clothes back on with no sign of his earlier embarrassment. Then, with a farewell salute, he jumped back into his car, fired up the engine and pulled out of the lay-by. As the car approached Terri and Lisa, the driver's window slid down. The man leaned out of the window and handed Terri a business card.

"See you around, girls," he winked and, with a roar from the engine, he sped off into the distance.

"Who is he?" said Lisa.

Terri looked down at the card. "It says, 'Mike Morgan, Car Valeting Service. Whenever. Wherever. We dance to your tune.'"

"Oh my God, do you think it wasn't his car?" said Lisa. "And he isn't rich?"

"Who knows," grinned Terri. "But I'm not complaining. He certainly danced to our tune."

Appointment with Theft

"Are you having a coronary?"

Small pieces of Albert's scone flew over the table cloth.

"What, dear?" Albert spluttered, dabbing at the spewed crumbs with his napkin whilst reluctantly looking away from the buxom young lady at the adjoining table.

"Your eyes are bulging."

"Are they? But there's nothing wrong with me. I was just thinking about…strawberries."

"Strawberries?"

"Yes…this is fine strawberry jam indeed. The best I've ever had!"

Martha sighed. Albert was so predictable. He could home in like a pigeon on any pair of breasts over a 36c. She'd never quite forgiven him for that moment at Brighton beach in 1965 when, after a whole day drooling like a rabid dog over Doris Fleming's bosom, Doris had slapped him across the cheeks.

Albert's obsession was humiliating, but at least it allowed Martha to focus on her own projects. Currently, her interest was solving mysteries. Detective work was very rewarding and she was becoming quite skilled at it. She'd already returned several lost gloves, found a stray poodle and reported several incidents of suspicious looking cars. She'd even witnessed Doris shoplifting at the chemists and, perhaps, taken rather too much delight in getting her arrested.

It was important for detectives to appear innocuous. Martha had, however, decided that she was simply not going to wear a silly tweed hat like Miss Marple. Her grey beret was infinitely better. She pulled it down further; it looked rather fetching with her matching grey mackintosh. She could almost be a secret agent.

"Are you having a stroke, Martha?"

"Pardon?"

"You're making some very strange faces. And you keep raising one eyebrow and twitching your mouth."

"Oh, don't be ridiculous, Albert. I was just thinking…what a lovely day it is for our anniversary coach trip."

"Really? You look like you're thinking about something else far more…"

"You're right," interrupted Martha. "This jam is delicious. It must be made homemade. It's as good as Lucy Avery's preserve which won first prize at the WI in 1974."

"Ah…Lucy," said Albert, reminiscing. It's twenty years since she passed on. Damn fine woman. Excellent strawberries…I mean strawberry jam."

Martha gazed over the restaurant veranda at the nearby park and surroundings whilst smiling inwardly at yet another of Albert's verbal faux pas. He'd never make a secret agent. She could imagine him being interrogated like Dustin Hoffman in Marathon Man. He'd submit at the merest mention of dental floss let alone a drill:

Oh God, not the floss. Anything but the floss! I'll tell you everything. My name is Albert. I have a wife, three children, seven grandchildren, two goldfish and I like women's breasts…

"Look over there!"

"What?" Martha coloured. She'd been so busy fantasising she'd forgotten to be observant. All the best detectives were observant.

"There's a youth climbing through that factory window!" said Albert, pointing over the veranda towards the industrial estate beyond the park boundary.

"Oh yes, I see him! Let's go down and see what he's up to."

"Don't be silly, dear. Let's call the police. They'll deal with it."

Albert emptied his pockets looking for his phone: wallet, handkerchief, indigestion tablets, penknife, a bottle of pills, an old tobacco tin containing his Fisherman's Friends and the compact camera the boys had bought for their anniversary which he had no idea how to use. But no phone. Where was it? Maybe he'd left it…

"Oh stop wasting time, Albert," said Martha. "I've got my phone so let's get down there. We can get a proper description."

"I'm not going. It's police work. You're just obsessed with spying."

"I'm not," said Martha, indignantly.

"You are. Every bloody night it's Agatha Christie or Murder, She Wrote. If I have to see Angela Lansbury feigning surprise one more time I'm going to top myself. And stop dressing like Miss Marple."

"I don't dress like Miss Marple. And I'm not spying, I'm merely observing."

"So that's what you call peeping between curtains and looking through keyholes."

"I don't."

"Oh yes you do."

"I do not! Anyway, how dare you ridicule me when, for the last forty years, I've put up with you eyeing up every pair of breasts within a ten mile radius."

"I don't."

"Oh yes you do."

"I do not!"

"You do. And I'm going down there whether you like it or not!"

Martha got up and marched down the steps from the veranda towards the factory. Albert pocketed his belongings and hurried after her. Martha was still as infuriating as the day he'd met her at the local am dram auditions. He'd been cast as Lord Fancourt Babberley in Charley's Aunt and she as his love interest. For three months she'd played coy, on and off the stage, and it hadn't been until the after-show party that he'd finally planted a proper smacker.

"Wait for me!" called Albert, catching up with Martha hiding behind a wall. "You could've waited. I could die being this short of breath."

"You get short of breath every time you see a picture of Oprah Winfrey."

"You're a heartless woman at times, Martha."

Martha ignored Albert's pitiful expression and peered round the wall.

"The door's ajar. He must've opened it ready for a quick getaway. Let's go in and see what he's doing."

"No way. He might be a druggie."

"Ssshh."

"Look, dear," said Albert, lowering his voice. "I don't want to end my days knifed by a teenage hoodlum. I want to die in my own bed."

"Hallucinating about vast breasts, I suppose," Martha whispered under her breath.

"What? Speak louder. You know my hearing's not so good."

"I said ruminating about last requests. You want to die ruminating about last requests."

"Yes, yes. Last requests. A double scotch perhaps. Maybe a cigar."

"Oh whatever, Albert. Now get out that camera, we're going in. Let's get some pictures."

"I can't work that new camera."

"Well, figure it out. The boys said it was easy to use. Now follow me."

Martha pulled open the door and tiptoed inside. Albert followed, fumbling with the camera. Once inside, they were surrounded by numerous rails of clothing and cardboard boxes packed almost to the ceiling. Martha grabbed Albert's arm and pulled him in between some garments so they were hidden from sight.

"I can't see him," whispered Martha, peering out between some clothes. "But I can hear movement from beyond that door."

"Oh my God!"

Martha looked at Albert. His face was as red as a plum tomato, sweat glistening on his forehead. "What's the matter?"

"It's…a…basque," whimpered Albert.

Martha examined the clothes hanging on the rails. They were crammed with hordes of ladies underwear: bras, knickers, petticoats and suspenders in almost every conceivable size, material and colour. And right at this very moment, Albert's nose was planted between two giant double D cups of a black leather basque. Martha looked at Albert's tortured face: it was like a drooling adolescent's not one of a man in his seventies. "Oh grow up, Albert," said Martha, kicking his shins. "And get ready with the camera."

Martha peeked back through the clothes just as the youth appeared in the room. He ransacked the desks, pulling out drawers and tipping them out over the floor. Unplugging some phones and a laptop computer, he paused briefly to admire them, and then shoved them in a holdall. Martha gestured to Albert for the camera. But he was still turning it over in his hands, bewildered.

"It's not working," said Albert breathlessly, as a bead of sweat dropped off his nose.

"Oh for goodness sake. You're useless. I'd better phone the police then," said Martha, opening her bag for her phone. She rummaged in its depths. But it wasn't there. She was sure she'd put in this morning. She looked again.

"It's not here," said Martha.

"Are you sure?"

"I put it in this morning. But now it's gone."

"You mean you forgot it. Your memory's going. Now look what a mess we're in."

"Nothing's wrong with my memory."

"Your memory's kaput, Martha. And your mind is going. The first stage of Alzheimers is believing you're a spy you know."

"What rubbish. Anyway, you can hardly talk. Where's your phone?"

"I don't care where it is. I'm dying," said Albert, wiping his sleeve across his brow. "My heart's beating too fast."

Martha studied Albert's troubled face and peeked back through the clothes again. "He's gone into another office.

Let's get out of here and sort you out then, you silly old codger."

Martha crept out of the building, pulling Albert by the sleeve. Outside, Albert gasped for breath, his chest heaving with exertion.

"Look, there's a bench opposite. Let's get you seated," said Martha.

"Give me my pills," said Albert as he slumped onto the seat.

"You don't need pills. You're just overexcited, Albert. You don't even have a heart condition."

"I need pills."

"For heaven's sake, you've just seen a few pairs of knickers," said Martha, handing him the bottle she'd extracted from his pocket. "Besides, these pills are for cholesterol."

"Look, there's your man," said Albert, unscrewing the bottle as the youth appeared outside the factory adjusting his bags.

"I've an idea," whispered Martha.

"Oh dear God," said Albert. "Not one of your ideas. I don't think I can take any more of your ideas."

"Just stay calm and play along. Remember your am dram days."

"God help me," said Albert and stuffed some pills into his mouth.

"Excuse me!" Martha shouted, waving at youth who glanced up from his bags for a moment. "Excuse me! Could you please help us?"

The youth lifted his head again but still appeared unwilling to help so Martha wiped her eyes and began to sniff. Reluctantly, the youth crossed the road towards them.

"I'm so sorry to trouble you," said Martha, letting her voice warble with distress. "I can see you're busy. Moving house?"

"Um…yeah. That's right," said the youth, clearly relieved Martha had provided him with an excuse for his numerous bags. "Moving in with my girlfriend."

"Oh, how delightful. You lucky young people. My husband and I have been together for forty years. In fact, it's forty years today." Martha took the youth aside. "My husband's not feeling so well though. It's his weak heart. Would you mind taking a photo of us? You know, just in case…it'd be such a shame not to have a memento of our special day."

"I dunno." The youth shifted his bags around impatiently. "I got things to do."

"Oh please, please. I'd be so grateful," pleaded Martha, giving Albert a wink.

"I really ain't got time, granny."

Martha winked desperately at Albert. As the youth turned away it finally clicked with Albert what Martha was up to and he started to cough and splutter.

"Oh no! I think he's having an attack!" howled Martha.

"I can't breathe!" said Albert, clutching his chest and rolling his head from side to side.

The youth stopped walking and looked back towards them.

"Oh please help," sobbed Martha. "Can you call the police?"

"You don't want the police," said the youth, alarmed. "You want an ambulance. Look, I'll take that photo and maybe he'll calm down."

"Oh you sweet, sweet boy," said Martha, pretending to wipe away her tears and turning back to Albert. "This lovely young man is going to take a photo of us. Have you got your camera, dear?"

"No idea how it works," gasped Albert dramatically, enjoying the ruse.

"No worries, guv. Got one of these myself."

"Oh my goodness, I don't think you'll manage that tiny camera with those leather gloves you've got on," said Martha.

"Yeah, you're right," replied the youth, slipping off his gloves and handing them to Martha, now sitting beside Albert. They held hands and smiled innocently. The youth looked down at the camera, flicked a couple of buttons and took a photo.

"Oh my goodness, that was so simple," said Martha, rising from her seat. "You are so clever. My husband has been trying to figure it out all day!"

"Easy when you know how," said the youth. "Here, you just open the shutter. Turn to "auto," focus and shoot. It does it all for you."

"You mean like this?" Martha took the camera from the youth's hands, placed it up to her eye and started taking photos…of Albert, the sky, the factory and finally the youth. She laughed delightedly. "This is amazing! We must take lots and lots of pictures of our special day, my dear. And thank you so much, young man, for helping us. You're so very, very kind."

"No worries," said the youth, accepting his gloves back from Martha and picking up his bags. "He looks okay now."

"Thanks to you," said Martha. "Have a lovely day with your girlfriend!"

Martha waved at the youth as he walked off down the road.

"You deceptive cow," said Albert.

"Yes, I was rather good, wasn't I?" replied Martha, glowing with pride.

"Bloody brilliant actually."

"Yes, I've his photo and his fingerprints. Miss Marple couldn't have done better!"

"I suppose not," Albert grinned. "And I'm feeling much better. Let's find a police station and then get back to the coach."

"Yes, let's go." Martha and Albert linked arms and headed back to the restaurant in amicable silence. After a few minutes, Albert pulled a lacy bra out of his pocket. "Look what I've got."

"Albert, you've stolen it!" said Martha, aghast at the sight of the underwear.

"Call it a reward. Besides, no one will miss it. It's tiny."

"What size is it?"

"A 34A."

"That's my size."

"I know."

"You're a very naughty man," said Martha, trying not to look pleased.

"I can't wait to get home," replied Albert. "Because you know what they say?"

"No," said Martha, even though she knew what was coming next.

"You can never keep a good man down."

Albert winked and put the bra back in his pocket.

Graveyard Tales

"Good Morning, Douglas. I see you're up to your neck in it."

"I didn't hear you sneaking up on me," said Douglas, tossing a shovelful of soil out of the grave and grinning as he saw Sister Lillian weaving her way through the headstones towards him.

"I doubt if I pretended I was the Lord Jesus rising from the dead that you'd be shocked," replied Sister Lillian, reaching the edge of the new grave and looking down at Douglas' handiwork. "I don't know how you do this job without getting the heebie jeebies."

Douglas took a breather and admired Sister Lillian's shapely legs which were uncommonly good for a woman of sixty-three.

"There's nothing that'll scare me," boasted Douglas, propping his spade up against a muddy embankment. "I've seen just about everything. Besides, I've the lovely

Sister Lily to bring me refreshments. What more could a man want?"

"Indeed," laughed Sister Lillian, passing down a mug of chocolate and a blueberry muffin which Douglas gratefully accepted.

"You know, I'll never forget when I put my foot through Montgomery's casket. It didn't scare me though, just caught me by surprise. I always said that family were cheapskates," said Douglas, sipping his steaming drink.

"Definitely. And between you and me,' said Sister Lillian leaning forward conspiratorially, "he never put more than a shilling in the plate!"

"Whole family were rotten misers," grumbled Douglas, taking a bite of his muffin.

"So, which of our beloved parishioners has gone to the dear Lord? A few days away and I've missed all the news."

"Well, Mr Perry popped his clogs from pneumonia on Friday: the funeral's tomorrow. And that one over there," Douglas pointed at a pile of earth covered in artificial grass further down the graveyard, "that one's for Willard. He had a heart attack on Thursday. He was eighty-nine: a right good innings. Funeral's this afternoon at two. I reckon there'll be a big turnout what with him ringing the bells for fifty years."

"I suppose Willard was ready enough, but poor Mr Perry. He was younger than both you and I. God rest his soul. Mrs Perry must be in a dreadful state."

"She's not so bad. But she wants a double 'un. So I gotta go down the best part of ten feet. It'll be an early night for me."

"Willard was lucky to live so long and with such good health," Sister Lillian reflected. "You know, I remember him getting up to mischief when he was young. He was such a handsome man and could be utterly charming."

"He wasn't called Willy Willard for nothing.'"

"Douglas! Remember, I am a virtuous lady," said Sister Lillian in mock horror.

"Don't I know it, Sister Lily. Never failed to be reminded of it when I see Him hanging around your neck."

"Now, now, Douglas. You mustn't be jealous," said Sister Lillian, touching the crucifix resting on her ample chest. "Remember good things come to those who wait."

Douglas pulled a regretful face and sipped his chocolate, knowing Sister Lily would always be out of his grasp. She would have been a corker in her day. If only he'd arrived in Castleridge with his adoptive parents before she'd taken her oaths.

"So what do you know about Willy Willard then?" said Douglas, trying to distract himself from Sister Lily's legs.

"Well, now he's gone, I don't suppose it can do any harm."

Sister Lillian checked over her shoulder and, as they were still alone, she lowered herself down onto the rim of the grave, dangling her feet into its depths.

"It was years ago, I was a slip of a girl and used to polish the church brass for pocket money. One day, I was climbing the bell tower and I smelt cigar smoke drifting down the staircase. Then I heard Willard's voice and a woman laughing and giggling… it wasn't his wife as I knew her well and used to run errands for her. I was so upset, I didn't know about things like that back then. It was all so shocking, I didn't know what to do…so I ran back down, crying like a fool."

"He was fornicating up the bell tower? Good Lord! No wonder he rang them bells for so many years!"

"But Willard…,"continued Sister Lillian, embellishing her story with relish, "he must have heard me crying. He chased after me, down the tower, across the altar, and caught me by my blazer. He begged me never to tell anyone…he said it was true love…that he couldn't help it. I didn't know what to believe but I never said anything. I was too scared."

"Sounds like Willard was a bit of a fella after all," said Douglas. "I bet he gave you a shock grabbing you like that, you being such a sweet young thing back then. 'Course, since you were corrupted by Him Upstairs no one's had a look in."

"That might change," said Sister Lillian, with a mischievous smile.

"What do you mean? Are you planning a date with the devil?"

"Not exactly."

"Bloody hell, you're not converting and becoming a vicar? Preaching from the pulpit and all that stuff?"

"Oh, don't be silly, Douglas. Once a Catholic, always a Catholic."

Douglas felt a tinge of disappointment. If Sister Lily was converting, he might have stood a chance with her but it was obviously one of her guessing games. She loved quizzes and crosswords more than any woman he knew.

"So, spit it out then, Lily. I've got a grave to dig and I've not got time for your nonsense today."

"Nonsense? Well now, perhaps you're not really interested…"

"Of course, I'm interested. But get on with it; if you were mine I'd have you over my knee for being such a frightful tease."

"Be careful what you say," said Sister Lillian, her eyes sparkling with humour.

"So?" said Douglas, moving nearer as his curiosity got the better of him.

"You know I was away for a few days? I went to see the Bishop and Sister Paula, the Mother Superior."

"And?" said Douglas, confused. He had no idea what Sister Lily's preamble was leading to.

"And…I am no longer a nun."

Douglas's mouth fell open. He clutched his chest anticipating a coronary.

"You…you…are no longer a nun?" stuttered Douglas.

"That's right."

"But…but…you've been a nun for forty years."

"It was time for a change."

"But how can you leave the order? It's been your life!"

"People change. I've devoted my best years to God but now I wish to devote the remainder of my earthly life to someone else. God is not an ogre. He understands more than you think."

"But what happens to you now? You'll have no home, nothing!" said Douglas, panicking at the thought of Lily thrown out from the convent.

"I'm not going to be cast out on the streets because I've left the order," replied Lily, soothingly. "I shall continue to teach and do many of the things I do for the parish – but not as a nun. Eventually, I will have to move out of the convent, of course. But I was sort of hoping I might get some offers of help…"

"What do you mean when you say you want to devote yourself to someone else?" interrupted Douglas, overcome with outrage at the thought of any other man being with his lovely Lily. "Have you been carrying on whilst you've been in the cloth?"

"For goodness sake, what kind of woman do you think I am, Douglas? Of course I haven't – there's only ever been one man, other than the Good Lord, who I've ever been interested in. Surely you know that?"

Unconsciously, Douglas gripped Lily's ankle. He felt the warmth of her flesh through her stockings, tingling in his fingers as the meaning of her words dawned on him.

"You're too late," said Douglas, looking mournfully up into Lily's eyes.

"I'm…I'm…too late?"

"Thirty odd years I've waited for you, Lily. I've passed over all the beauties and stayed a bachelor because I loved you. Even when I was with other girls, I thought of you. But yesterday…I promised myself to Mrs Perry."

"But Mr Perry only died last week!"

"I thought I should make up for lost time."

"But…that's outrageous. And I've loved you for nearly thirty years!"

"So you have, have you?" said Douglas with a wicked grin, jerking Lily's ankle so that she slipped down into the grave, where he pinned her up against the muddy bank. "Well now I'm marrying Mrs Perry - so that'll teach you to keep a man waiting for thirty years."

"You're lying aren't you?" said Lily, her voice quavering, not quite sure if Douglas was teasing her but unable to focus on anything but his devilish eyes.

"Yes, I am."

Douglas brushed his lips gently against Lily's.

"Thirty years I've dreamt of this moment, Lily. Thirty years I've loved you from a distance, believing I would never hold you in my arms, never kiss you. It's been a living hell. And now you say you love me…"

"We can make up for it."

"That's a lot of making up and making out to make up for thirty years abstinence, you know."

"We can try," said Lily, a tear running down her cheek.

"Best get started then," said Douglas clamping his mouth on Lily's.

"Douglas! This is the churchyard!" squealed Lily.

"Sometimes a man's gotta do what a man's gotta do. And I've waited thirty years. Nothing's gonna stop me know!" said Douglas, running his tongue over Lily's lips and letting his hand stray towards her breasts. He could feel her heart pounding beneath his palm, her soft welcoming mouth.

"Douglas, are you sure here is the right place?" said Lily, tearing her lips away.

"Have mercy on me, Lily. If we don't make love now I shall explode," pleaded Douglas, looking down at his trousers. "I'm like a jet propelled missile."

Lily looked down and saw a huge bulge in Douglas' trousers. Then, daringly, she placed her hand over it. "It moves."

"Of course it moves. What do you think it does?"

"I don't know…I don't know how these things work. I'm a nun."

"Correction. You were a nun and now you're my wife to be and I'm going to educate you. Right this is…" Douglas looked down at the gigantic stiff in his pants and seemed lost for words. "This is…my…my…manhood."

"Your manhood? Isn't that a bit old fashioned?"

"Look, exactly how much do you know?"

"Not much."

"Right, I'll keep it simple then. This is my manhood and it moves. Usually I make it move but then sometimes…it does its own thing."

"Not in church I hope."

"You're going to get a spanking in a minute."

"Douglas! Remember I am a virgin."

Douglas clasped his hands together in prayer, closed his eyes and began to mutter.

"Not in my wildest, wildest dreams have I dreamt this. I'm finally getting to make out with the woman I love who, not only is a nun, but a virgin. Dear God, you've kept me waiting for such a long, long time but I thank you from the very bottom of my heart."

"Um…Douglas. The lesson?" interrupted Lily.

"Yes, yes. Right, so this is my manhood," said Douglas opening his eyes, "And these are…your breasts!"

"I know they're my breasts. What do you think?" giggled Lily.

Douglas stood in awe gaping at Lily's breasts bulging over a large wired bra as she pushed them towards him.

"Oh my God, they are magnificent, Lily. Magnificent! The best pair of boobs I have ever seen!"

"Now you're exaggerating, Douglas. They're good but not that good."

"Believe me, Lily, they are bloody marvellous," grinned Douglas. "Can I touch them?"

"Since you're now my husband to be, I suppose that's all right," said Lily shyly, her cheeks flushing pink.

Douglas leaned forward and gently touched the curve of Lily's left breast as he ran his other hand up between her thighs.

"Bloody hell, what's going on down there?" said Douglas, pulling away and hitching up Lily's pleated navy skirt. "What the hell are these?"

"My thermals," replied Lily, looking down at her pink long johns.

"Thermals. Over…tights?"

"It's cold."

"So thermals, tights and, presumably…knickers?"

"Yes. I like to feel…safe."

"What from…a panzer tank?"

"Douglas!"

"We shall have to do something about this. I can't have a wife who wears old maid's undies. Right, let's be getting them off."

"I can't take off my underwear in the church yard!"

"Of course, you can, Lily. Besides, we're almost married now. The vows are just a formality."

Douglas slipped his fingers over the waistband of her thermals and tights and started to pull them down.

"Jesus Christ. It's like Second Front," said Douglas, struggling with thermals, now stuck half way down Lily's thighs.

"I'm not sure this is a good idea," said Lily, anxiously.

"Trust me, my love, we're perfectly safe. This is not the job where you get a lot of onlookers. Right, there you go. I'll leave them around your ankles – them you can hitch them up fast if we do hear anyone."

"This is not quite how I imagined our first romantic encounter," said Lily looking bemused at the thermals and tights bunched up around her feet.

"I've left your knickers on: I don't want you getting a chill before I've warmed you up."

"Why, thank you, Douglas. And to think I gave up the nunnery for you. What was I thinking of?"

"We were destined to be together, my love," said Douglas, beaming.

"I know," replied Lily. "It just took me a while to figure it out."

"Thirty years, even for a woman to figure something out, must be a record," grinned Douglas. "Anyway, I'm going to show you what you've been missing."

Douglas began to stroke Lily again over the top of her knickers.

"Now, my Lily, Lesson Number Two: you need to stroke my head."

Douglas tensed involuntarily in anticipation. He felt Lily's hands begin to stroke his head. And his nose. And his ears.

"You have lovely hair. And hardly any grey. And your ears are so small," said Lily with affection.

"Not that head. The other one!" said Douglas.

"What other one? You've only got one head, Douglas. Oh dear, maybe this has all been too much for you…"

"Oh, my God, I don't believe this!" said Douglas, raising his eyes in despair. "A head…well a head is also a nickname for…well, you know…"

"No, I don't."

"The end bit of that bit down there," said Douglas, eyeing up the bulge in his trousers again.

"Oh, I see," exclaimed Lily, her eyes following Douglas's gaze.

"Thank God for that."

"I really am out of touch aren't I?"

"Not to worry, my Lily," grinned Douglas. "I would've been worried if you'd been reading Cosmopolitan instead of your missal every night."

"Shall we try again then?" said Lily, gaining confidence. "Maybe you should take off your trousers?"

Douglas eagerly unzipped his trousers and pulled them down. "I need to take my boots off. Just move along a bit so I've got more room."

Douglas bent over to take off his boots as Lily moved down the grave, forgetting her tights were round her ankles.

"Ahhh," screamed Lily as she tripped over her tights and fell headlong into the grave.

"What is it, what's the matter?" said Douglas, looking up and catching a foot in his trousers and tumbling on top of Lily.

"Uhhh," mumbled Lily, now covered in the mud and squashed beneath Douglas.

"Are you alright?"

"Well I was, till you landed on me," said Lily, spitting out some dirt.

"Sorry. I'll move."

Douglas pushed himself up on his elbows and yelled. "Ahhh!"

"What, what is it?"

"Fucking spade just landed on my head."

"Which head?"

"Don't try and be clever," said Douglas, rubbing his head and sitting up.

Lily pulled herself up and turned around to face Douglas.

"You know, I think God's trying to tell us something here."

"You could be right, my love," said Douglas grinning. "Although, I don't think anything else could possibly get between us now."

"Douglas, Douglas! Are you all right?" called a voice across the churchyard.

"Oh dear, it's Father Patrick," said Lily, hurriedly hoisting up her tights.

"Don't move!" whispered Douglas, jumping to his feet as best he could with his trousers still in disarray. He popped his head up over the side of the grave; Father Patrick was marching across the churchyard. Douglas put up his hand to halt him.

"I wouldn't come any closer, Father."

"Is everything all right, Douglas? I thought I heard screaming."

"I just found something gruesome that's all, Father."

"Do you…need some help?" stuttered Father Patrick already looking ashen and queasy at the thought of having to assist Douglas.

"No, no. It's nothing for you to worry about, Father. You go back to work and I'll sort it out. It just took me surprise that's all."

"Right, right," replied Father Patrick, trying to disguise his relief. "Are you absolutely sure?"

"Absolutely, Father. No problem."

Douglas watched Father Patrick turn hastily around and hurry back to the presbytery.

"Phew, that was close," said Douglas, sinking back down into the grave.

"You lied to him" said Lily.

"No, I didn't" said Douglas, picking a monstrous worm of his shirt and dangling it in front of Lily's face. "Look at the size of that bugger. Like a fucking python!"

"You know, I really do think God's trying to tell us something here," said Lily.

"I know, I know. I suppose I can wait till we're married."

"I love you, Douglas."

"I love you too."

Douglas kissed Lily gently on the lips and then he leaned back and looked into her eyes.

"So how about next week then?"

"Why not?" smiled Lily. "We've waited long enough."

"After all these years, I'll finally have someone to call "family," said Douglas. "It's been a while since my parents passed on. I've been on my own a long time."

"But now you'll have me," said Lily, returning Douglas's kiss.

"I tell you, Mona, I feel like I've been here all my life," said a loud voice, carrying across the empty graveyard.

"Jesus. What now?" said Douglas, reluctantly pulling away from Lily's parted lips and zipping up his trousers.

"It's a pity we never got to meet Willard but at least I got to know the truth," said the approaching voice.

"The truth will always out," replied a woman. "That's what my mother used to say."

"Hello, hello. What have we here? Another grave. Looks like some other poor bugger has snuffed it," said the man's voice.

"Oh don't go over, Jim. It's just a hole. Let's go and warm up in the car before the service."

"Just a minute. I've always been fascinated by graves. Interested party I guess," laughed the man. "This one looks like it might be double 'un."

Douglas looked up just as a man appeared on top of the mound of earth piled by the graveside. Lily backed away trying to look inconspicuous as the man stared down into the dark recesses.

"Oh, my God," said the stranger.

"Oh, my God," said Douglas.

"Bloody hell," exclaimed the stranger.

"Bloody hell," exclaimed Douglas.

"Who are you?" said the stranger, turning white.

"Who are you?" replied Douglas

"Watch out, Jim. You're slipping!" screamed Mona.

"Watch out, Douglas. He's slipping!" echoed Lily.

The stranger swayed for a moment and toppled forward. There was a yell, a thud and then it all went quiet.

Douglas opened his eyes. The sky above him was a fuzzy blue and the sound of piped organ music rang in his ears. His body felt weighted down and his legs trapped.

"I'm dead," he groaned.

"Are you alright, Douglas?" said Lily, squashed up against the far wall of the grave. "I can't get to you."

"I can't move," groaned Douglas.

"Can you wiggle your toes?" said an anxious woman's voice.

Douglas tried to wiggle in his toes inside his big sturdy boots.

"Aye, I think so."

"We'll get you out in a jiffy, Douglas," said Father Patrick, peering over the edge of the grave. "The Paramedics will be here in just a moment."

"Ughhh," moaned a voice.

A head rose from its resting place on Douglas's stomach and flopped down again.

"Ahhhh," screamed Douglas, seeing the stranger and trying to pull himself away. "A ghost!"

"It's alright. It's my husband," cried the now familiar voice of the woman "He's fallen in on top of you. Try and push him to one side a bit. He's coming around now."

The stranger groaned again.

"Jim, Jim… are you alright?" said the woman, leaning over the edge of the grave.

A face appeared above Douglas again, followed by the torso and arms of a short, stocky man. Douglas screamed even louder.

"Ahhhhhh!"

"Ahhhhhhhh!" screamed Jim in reply.

"It's me!" said Douglas.

"It's me!" said Jim.

"I'm dead," yelled Douglas.

"I'm dead," yelled Jim.

"Excuse me," interrupted Father Patrick from his graveside vigil. "Now may God forgive me for taking his name in vain. But, Jesus Christ, you two are you two a pair of stupid fuckers. You're obviously brothers. Twin brothers."

"It certainly looks that way," said Lily, looking from one identical face to the other.

"Oh my goodness, this is so exciting," said the woman. "We knew Jim had a twin. But we couldn't trace him. And now we come to his father's funeral and we find him. And not only that but his brother's an identical twin!"

"His father's funeral? said Lily.

"Why, yes. William Willard was Jim's father. But we only found out two weeks ago and by the time we'd made our arrangements to travel here, we heard he was dead. It's so sad that after all these years they never got to meet. But now we've found Jim's brother. Oh this is so exciting!"

"You're my brother?" said Douglas.

"Yep, looks like it," said Jim, rubbing his head.

"And Willard is my father?" said Douglas.

"No doubt about it," said Jim. "He got some floozy pregnant and we were adopted."

"Oh, my God," said Douglas. "I thought I had no family."

"God ain't got anything to do with it, bro. Our Willy was a randy old bugger."

Two paramedics appeared at the edge of the grave and in a short while the two men were hauled to the top and being checked over.

"You know," said Lily to Douglas and Jim when the paramedics had left. "How old are you two?"

"Fifty-seven," said Jim and Douglas in unison.

"That would make your births the year I saw Willard up the bell tower. It's all coming together now."

Douglas, Jim, Lily, Mona, Father Patrick and the large party of now confused parishioners who had come for Willard's funeral made their way across the graveyard to the church.

"So, you're a grave digger then?" said Jim, turning to Douglas.

"Aye, that I am, Jim. And you?"

"I'm a funeral director."

"Never!" said Douglas.

"Well," said Jim, wrapping his arm around Douglas and laughing. "We'd better go into partnership."

"Aye, indeed," said Douglas, grinning. "And to think I thought I had no family and now I've got a wife-to-be, a brother and a sister-in-law. I'm a lucky man."

"You are indeed, Douglas," said Father Patrick. "They say the Lord moves in mysterious ways but I have to say this is one of his more curious ones."

Father Patrick closed the church door behind his flock. He knew that families came in many shapes and forms and, as the organist began to play, he acknowledged that Douglas's new family was probably going to be a strange but rather special one.

Salty

A Modern Life

There are no mirrors in the bedroom but Jenny still lowers her head so her hair covers her face. Rob thrusts harder, squeezing her breasts.

"Spread your legs wider."

Jenny follows his instructions, her four inch heels sinking deep into the carpet. Her legs are so far apart it's uncomfortable, the pressure against her small frame overbearing. She exhales again at the sheer force of Rob's weight. It excites him so he rises up over her and forces her down onto the bed so she is sprawled out before him. Jenny stretches out her arms, clutches the bedspread and rotates her hips. She knows it is pleasing for him to see her subjugated beneath him.

Rob's pounding is incessant and furious. Jenny knows the rules so she raises her bottom to meet him as he grips her hips. He shudders, thrusts one more time and Jenny feels him pulsating within her, the energy slowly draining out of him. He flops down on her for a moment, enjoying his release. She struggles for breath, her face compressed into the duvet. Then Rob pulls away, slapping her buttocks.

"You're one hot fuck," he says and heads off into the ensuite shower.

Jenny lies still and studies the roses on the linen. Subtle shades of pink and yellow. Moss coloured stems and leaves. Small, sharp thorns. A tear slips silently down her nose. She wipes it away with her finger as she hears squabbling. She rolls over and reaches for her knickers discarded on the floor, uneasy at the children's proximity.

"So what are you up today?" says Rob reappearing from the bathroom, a towel wrapped round his waist.

"Nothing much, just the usual."

"Great stuff," says Rob, eyeing up his array of ties.

At eight o'clock Rob reverses out of the driveway in his sleek, black car. Jenny picks up the phone and dials the school.

"Hello, it's Mrs Rowan. I'm very sorry both Maddie and Josh have come down with a bug. They won't be in for the last two days of term."

Jenny replaces the phone, fetches a pen and paper from a drawer, sits down at the kitchen table and begins to write.

* * * * *

Rob stares at the tanned legs in front of him, long and athletic. He appreciates legs in heels but also in trainers. So much depends on height. Unconsciously, he pulls back his shoulders and straightens his spine.

"I won't be long. Then we can get started. Just ran ten miles in one hour twenty two. Would have been quicker but the roads were shit."

Rob looks over the rim of his glasses again, watching Matt adjust the digital display on his watch as sweat trickles down his inner thighs. He imagines Matt in the shower, sponging them. An email pings and Rob looks down at his screen, his thoughts instantly replaced by curiosity about his incoming correspondence. Matt coughs and Rob looks up again.

"So, do you think I can break the one twenty barrier before the marathon?"

"I don't see why not," says Rob, playing the game. "Look how well you've improved in sixth months. You're a natural runner. You've got the legs for it."

Matt grins and looks down at his legs.

"Yeah, the ladies seem to like them too."

"There's no accounting for taste," grins Rob. "I was a full back in my day and I was never short of a date."

"Is that how you met Jenny? Was she a groupie?"

"No chance. There's cheap dates and class acts. Jen's a class act."

"Well, see you in five," says Matt, turning abruptly towards the door. "Gotta get cleaned up. Let's tackle the Dock project first. We need to sort out that tosser, Jon Andrews. Any more calls from him and I'll lose my rag."

Rob nods in acknowledgement and opens the email as Matt closes the door; it's trivial nonsense from HR. He deletes it and resumes thinking about Matt's legs, strong and agile. Runners' legs. He looks at Jenny's photograph on his desk. It's his favourite picture of her; sitting on a river bank, legs sleek and slender, drawn up beneath her chin.

Rob opens up his folders and looks for Matt's report. At thirty-four Matt has it made: money, women, cars. He's also the Chief Executive's son. A healthy position to be in. It doesn't worry Rob that technically Matt's his superior because everyone knows it's Rob who calls the shots. Matt isn't stupid though. In fact, he's pretty clever and certainly smart enough to know that when Rob tells him what to do he should do it. So the CEO is happy, Matt's happy and, most importantly, Rob's happy taking home his huge pay packet.

Rob opens the Dock project file and starts to read, taking the occasional sip of black coffee from a porcelain teacup and saucer that sit next to his laptop. Rob finds mugs distasteful. They irritate him, especially when he sees their circular stains on his colleagues' expensive desks. He runs his finger slowly around the rim of his cup, delighting in its smoothness. It's a favourite that Jenny bought him. He's never mentioned his dislike of mugs yet they don't have any at home, not even one with World's Best Husband or Greatest Dad on it.

The coffee chills as Rob lingers on the conclusions of Matt's report. It's thorough and perceptive. Matt can identify problems easily but finds it harder to offer solutions and Rob knows solutions don't always jump out at you. Sometimes they resemble an intricate game of chess with short, interim and long term objectives that require meticulous planning. Rob is more of a solutions man himself and, luckily for him, it is the solutions man that usually takes the credit.

Matt returns as Rob is refilling his cup from the cafetiére. He pours Matt one too and as he passes it to him he notices Matt's choice of clothes: a pale lilac shirt and contrasting striped purple tie. Rob prefers more conservative choices but the colours work well on Matt with his light grey suit and youthful looks. There's only ten years' age difference between them but Rob acknowledges that Matt's generation seem far more fashion conscious and all together more modern.

"So what shall we do about Jonathan? The man is driving me insane. Any ideas?" says Matt, taking a seat and stretching out his long legs.

"Indeed, I do," says Rob. "In six months he'll be begging for us to buy him out."

"Just what I like to hear," grins Matt in return. "Details?"

Rob laughs and wonders why Matt comes into his office every morning and tells him his run time. It's a bit inconvenient but, then again, he does always enjoy his company.

* * * * *

"Flight EJ206 to Athens is now boarding at gate two."

Jenny picks up her holdall and passes Maddie and Josh their rucksacks.

"Not long now and we'll be on our way."

"Are you sure Daddy won't mind us going without him?" says Maddie, trying to hide her excitement but still anxious about her father's absence.

"Sweetheart, I told you; Daddy's got an extremely busy week. It's almost the end of term and you've both done incredibly well so we thought an extra special reward was called for."

"It'll still be odd without Daddy."

"He doesn't mind at all and I'm sure he'd want you to have loads of fun."

"Will there be a swimming pool?" says Josh.

"You bet!" says Jenny. "Now let's get going. We don't want to miss our flight."

Jenny doesn't like lying and today has been full of lies. First to the school receptionist, then to the neighbours and now to the children. But the letter, that wasn't lies. It just told the truth. Jenny knows that sometimes the truth hurts.

* * * * *

Jenny rests on the sunbed, a slow, creeping tiredness beginning to seep through her limbs. She half opens her eyes, hidden behind dark glasses, and checks on Maddie and Josh. They've found some other children to play with and are jumping noisily in and out of the pool. The lifeguard seems alert so Jenny relaxes again, flicks her eyes shut and clears all her negative thoughts. She concentrates on the sun warming her bones, the water trickling in the fountain and imagines swimming naked in the sea, soft waves lapping over her.

"Excuse me, is this lounger taken?"

Jenny jolts out of her slumber, opens one eye and squints at the man standing in between her and the adjacent sunbed. He's about six foot with greying black hair, a gentle brown tan and a pleasant, friendly face. Jenny takes off her glasses, greasy from suntan lotion, for a closer inspection. It probably seems rude but she doesn't care. She looks him up and down and decides he seems genuine, not the obvious sexual predator wanting to ogle her legs.

"Just need a quieter spot," he says, seeming to read her thoughts.

Jenny knows he doesn't have to ask. She could tell another lie if she wanted but she doesn't want to. She's fed up with lying.

"It's free. Be my guest," she says with a small, welcoming gesture.

"You're English," he says, throwing his towel over the lounger and sitting down on its edge.

"Can I just say now," says Jenny turning towards him and looking him straight in the eye. "I'm not related to the Queen, I don't drink tea and I detest cucumber sandwiches." Jenny pauses and put her glasses back on. "Although I do like cucumber in a salad."

There's a brief silence and then the man's laughter rings out, deep and loud. Jenny spontaneously smiles.

"I'm American. From California."

Jenny watches him rub sun lotion over his chest. It's a hairy chest but not unpleasantly hairy.

"I'd noticed."

He looks up as if he didn't expect a reply and smiles.

"The accent, huh?"

"No. The shorts."

He looks down at his shorts, confused.

"Hawaii-Five-0. So passé," says Jenny.

He laughs again and Jenny notices the way his eyes laugh too.

"You're right. Probably not the most fetching swimwear," he muses. "Actually, I prefer Speedos but I'm a modest kind of guy. Don't like to attract attention to myself."

Jenny giggles at his innuendo and leans back on her sunbed again. She hears the plastic creak beneath his weight as he gets comfortable. They lie in mutual silence as the sun beats down. Jenny dozes off and wakes only when she feels a smooth, cold tickle on her leg which sends an unexpected shiver down her spine.

"Drink, honey?"

The American is standing next to her holding up an iced glass, a cocktail umbrella sticking up high and proud.

"Honey?" she murmurs.

"An Americanism."

"It's a nice Americanism." She reaches out and takes the glass. "Thank you."

Later that night, Jenny clasps her legs around his buttocks and pulls him in. His eyes are a startling blue. She realises it's a long time since she's seen Rob's eyes up close.

"You know, Honey, I don't normally do this."

"Me neither."

They examine every aspect of each other's faces. Eyes, noses, lips. Then they kiss, cheek to cheek, mouth to mouth, tongue to tongue. Jenny draws her legs higher around his back as he pushes inward. They lie entwined, barely moving.

"You're a beautiful, wonderful woman," he whispers.

Jenny holds his gaze and sees his sincerity. It feels good. She can't remember the last time she felt so close to someone, even though they barely know each other. She wishes the moment would last longer but knows it can't. But as pleasure courses throughout her mind and body she doesn't feel any guilt, only freedom.

* * * * *

Rob sits with his back to his desk, watching seagulls surf on the crest of the wind. His emails are unanswered and his coffee is cold. He wonders what it would be like to be a bird, wild and free, soaring high as small black figures rush to and fro beneath him in the squalor of the city. A bird flies close to the window, squawks and draws his attention back to the letter. He reads it for the sixth time that morning. He spent all weekend reading it too, turning the pages over and over in bewilderment, hoping the words would fall into place. But they don't and in the early hours of Monday morning he falls asleep, his breath stale with whiskey, his pillow damp with tears. He doesn't fully understand the letter but he does know that everything he had, he may lose.

"One hour nineteen!" exclaims Matt, rushing into Rob's office, an arm held high in triumph.

Rob says nothing, does nothing. His mind is still fixated on the letter.

"Mate?"

Rob awakes from his trance and swivels slowly around in his chair. Matt's never seen Rob look so rough, his face grey and drawn. He searches his mind for the exact word to describe Rob - melancholic. That's it. He's never seen Rob look so melancholic.

"What's up?" says Matt taking his usual seat. "Want to tell me about it?"

Rob tosses the letter across to Matt and stares sullenly into space. Matt reads it twice, his heart picking up speed as the words form sentences and the sentences form meaning.

"She wants a divorce," says Rob.

"It doesn't actually say that."

"It's implied."

"Possibly, but not definitively."

"What the hell does that mean?"

"Well it's clear she thinks there's something going on with you and you don't love her anymore. Anything else is open for questions."

"That's completely untrue! I adore her!"

"Adoration isn't the issue, Rob."

"What do you mean?"

"Love, adoration: they're different things."

"I could lose everything. The house. The kids."

"You're overreacting, Rob. They're no threats here. You're not going home to find your clothes hacked or have your cock cut off in the night."

Rob snorts.

"Well not at least till she gets back from Athens."

"It's breathing space. Time to think things through."

"I don't understand. I thought everything was perfect."

"And that's why you need to think. Because clearly it's not."

Rob goes off into a trance again. Matt makes Rob a fresh cup of coffee and puts it next to his laptop.

"Drink this. Think it through. Write down your thoughts and maybe then it will become clearer. I'll have your calls re-routed to my office."

Rob looks at Matt and smiles weakly.

"Thanks, mate."

"You're a solutions man, Rob. But you need to find your problem first. And I can't help you with this one."

* * * * *

Matt bites into his prawn and salad sandwich. The BLT was more tempting but the two hundred extra calories seemed indulgent. But now, as the sandwich tastes bland and dry, Matt chucks it impulsively into the bin. He opens a drawer and takes out a giant sized Mars Bar and revels in the sticky chocolate and caramel.

He didn't realise Rob did so much work. He's been fielding Rob's calls all morning and it's been non-stop aggravation. Sometimes he's even had to find impromptu answers. No wonder Rob didn't have a clue what was happening at home; his mind must be on the go continuously, dreaming up solutions, worrying about profits and shareholders. Getting fucked up with speeches and conferences and God knows what else. It's no surprise really that Jenny doesn't think Rob loves her anymore - and why Rob doesn't know what's going on inside his own head.

Matt screws the wrapper up and flicks it across the room. Sometimes life is crap. He opens the contact list on his phone. He has two tickets for the theatre tonight and he needs a partner. He scrolls down his list, looking for someone suitable. Sherrie always enjoys the theatre but he took her last week and he doesn't want to get serious. Ditto Lucy. Fran he knows has a date already and Jules is on holiday. He could ask Linda from Marketing who looks the part but she might get too keen too soon.

Matt sighs and closes his contacts. It doesn't seem right to go out when Rob is so miserable. He dials him on his mobile. No answer. He dials again.

"Rob Rowan."

"Hi Rob. It's me. How are you feeling?"

"Pretty pathetic."

"Oh," Matt pauses. "Look, I was just wondering if you could use some company tonight? A friendly ear."

Silence. He can almost hear Rob weighing up the pros and cons before he speaks. Matt finds himself holding his breath.

"Okay, Matt. Thanks. Much appreciated."

"I'll drop by when we shut up shop."

Matt puts the phone back down. He realises he is sweating. He wipes the sweat from his upper lip and wonders if Rob has figured anything out.

* * * * *

They stand on the steps, holding hands and smiling. They look great together. Better than great. Maybe perfect. If such a thing exists. Jenny notices the occasional dispassionate glances of pedestrians as a gust of wind blows confetti across the street and acknowledges that marriage isn't the institution it was. She doesn't know if that's good or bad or neither. If it were multiple choice she'd tick "Don't know."

"I'll walk," says Jenny as Josh and Maddie leap into the limousine with Rob and Matt. Rob nods. Things might have changed but they still share some understanding and appreciation.

Jenny figures she won't be missed at the reception for at least an hour and slips away into the busy, cosmopolitan streets of London. Garish adverts, burger wrappers and shops displaying gaudy bling line the streets. Today, everything seems louder, brighter and more vibrant. Jenny doesn't know why. But she does know that for good, for bad, for better, for worse, everything changes.

It is, after all, a modern life.

The Princess and the Thief

Mummy ran out the back door, Daddy ran out the front door. I think they forgot about me.

Daddy's a banker. He travels a lot. Mummy said this time he'd gone too far. She threw the earrings he'd bought her in the bin. Then Daddy threw his briefcase across the kitchen. It hit Mummy's china.

I took my parcel into the lounge and cried.

The string on my parcel is too tight. I need scissors from the kitchen. It's messy in there. Perhaps Mummy and Daddy will be pleased if I tidy up. So I pick Mummy's earrings out of the bin and put them in her special cookie jar and I put Daddy's briefcase back on the table.

Daddy calls me his Princess and Mummy calls me her Angel.

I collect the big pieces of the broken plates and drop them in the bin. There's a shadow on the floor, I look up and see a man staring through the window. I know him but I can't remember his name. I saw him outside the school gates last week. He waves at me. I wave back.

He opens the porch door and smiles.

"Can I help? You don't want to cut yourself."

"If you like," I say.

"I saw your parents leave, so I thought I'd better check on you. I was right to be concerned; I see there's been an accident."

"I don't think Daddy meant to break Mummy's china. He was cross because Mummy said he loves money more than he loves us."

"I'm sure he doesn't."

He finds the broom and starts to sweep the pieces into little piles.

"I think your daddy knows how important money is to live. But your mummy knows other things are even more important. Like children." He smiles again and pushes the little piles into one big mound and I brush it into the dustpan. "It's a question of finding the right balance."

He smiles again and I smile back.

"Daddy brought me a present. It's in the lounge."

"Well, we're just about done here. Shall we go and take a look?"

I shake the pieces out of the dustpan into the bin and take the scissors from the drawer.

"Lead on my Merry Mistress!" he says. "Let's find the hidden treasure!"

He smiles and laughs all the time. He reminds me of Santa Claus, only he doesn't have a beard.

I cut the string, rip off the paper and open the box.

"Wow, look at that!" he says. "It's the biggest book I've ever seen! The Princess and the Thief. It sounds exciting."

I trace my fingers over the large, gold letters.

"Daddy always buys beautiful presents."

"Shall I read or do you want to?" he says.

"I'll read."

He closes his eyes. He looks peaceful and content like Daddy does after Sunday lunch. Sometimes I don't know a word, so I spell it out loud and he tells me what it is. He would be a good teacher as he is very patient. I read on until the story ends.

He opens his eyes and smiles again.

"You have a lovely, soothing voice and read so well."

"Will I meet a prince?"

"Every girl meets her prince."

He holds out his hand and leads me to the window. The sky is blue and sunny but he tells me how clouds form and why rain falls.

"Shall we go for a walk?" he says. "While the weather's good?"

"What about Mummy and Daddy?"

"We could leave a note."

"Can I bring my storybook?"

"That's a wonderful idea."

I begin to write a message on my pink notepad.

"What's your name?" I say.

He leans over and looks at my writing.

"Just put you're going for a walk with your prince," he winks.

I like my prince. He is charming. He is kind.

I finish my note and put it in the centre of the table. My prince picks up my storybook and takes me by the hand. We walk through the house and out onto the pavement.

"There are clouds on the horizon," he says. "Let's take my car to the park."

I climb in and we drive down the avenue. I look back through the rear window and see Mummy running down the street waving at me as a big drop of water falls on the glass.

It begins to rain.

No Returns

I'd never stolen anything before. Honest. It was the first time. I guess there's a first time for everything. A first time for living, and a first time for dying.

It slipped silently into my pocket. No one saw, no one ever does. Least of all him. I don't exist as me. Just a useful puppet. A puppet with broken strings.

It's lavender fragrance. "Calming" it says on the bottle. It swirls, blends with the steaming water. The deep purple essence dilutes to shades of lilac bindweed, warm, inviting.

My fleshy thighs fade to shapeless shadows. My breasts lie flat. No more womanly curves. Just an amorphous being who cooks, cleans, and draws clouds in the dust.

Water trickles down the overflow. I don't suppose many people have a waterfall for a requiem.

The bottle sits on the shelf, carton discarded. The scent spirals upwards, weaving its way to freedom. If only I could escape my box so easily. Climb free, run wild. But I'm sealed with Sellotape and tied with string.

The water creeps into my ear, my head lolls. I feel relaxed, sleepy. Sometimes it can be quite cosy in my box. I hear small muffled voices. Crying, laughing. It's just a trick. But it makes me wonder. Wonder whether I should sleep or not. Bubbles in my nostrils. Only a moment longer now. I could hook my leg over the edge...or welcome the embrace.

But whatever I choose, there'll be no return.

The Fisherman, his Rod, his Wife and her Sandwich

It was the hottest day of the year. Even under the shade of my umbrella the heat was unbearable. I'd discarded my shirt by mid-morning, wading into the water in just my shorts and plimsolls. Casting my rod out, I'd watched the multi-coloured fly skim across the surface of the river whilst the waters slipped silently past.

Like my life.

It was peaceful here. Sheer heaven. Free from Gilda and her constant nagging: "Do this, do that. Clean the car, empty the bins, paint the kitchen, and don't forget to mow the grass before your mother comes."

Oh yes, and kiss my arse.

It was hard to believe Gilda was the same woman I'd married long ago with a smile that greeted me daily as I arrived home from my job with the council. How things change. Maybe I hadn't been ambitious enough. My job cleaning windows wasn't great. But it was reliable. It wasn't like I was self-employed and the income irregular. There was always money to put food on the table and for holidays. Okay, so we hadn't had holidays to the Caribbean but we'd always had them: a beach in Spain; a villa in Portugal; a gite in France. We even went to Venice for our honeymoon.

At first we'd had a lot in common. Gilda had been a sales assistant at Little Women, a clothing chain for petite women. Nothing grand. We lived a simple life during the week but on the weekends we partied or went to the cinema and, whilst I went fishing on Sundays, Gilda seemed content to do her own thing. It all seemed quite perfect and I never felt the need to become chief window cleaner or look for another job. It wasn't that I'd never had aspirations but, as I passed from my twenties into my thirties and no kids arrived, there didn't seem the urgency to progress. With no extra mouths to feed and no need to buy the latest fashionable trainers, I suppose I just became content with what I'd got.

Gilda had gone through a broody stage though. We'd tried homeopathic remedies for conception, special diets and ovulation temperature gauges. Gilda had even tried handstands against the bedroom wall. "Anything's worth a try," she'd say, her long blonde hair trailing over her face. I watched at first; her slim agile legs splayed against the flowered wallpaper and her breasts, round and firm, with nipples still engorged from our lovemaking. But as the months passed it became increasingly tedious. My advances were counteracted by; "You've had your lot. A week on Tuesday and I'll be fertile. Let's save it for then." Eventually, we went to the doctors; I with my sperm sample in hand and her with a chip on her shoulder.

It turned out that I had a low sperm count. I wasn't barren but instead of fifty million plus of the little fellas, I only had about forty million and some of the buggers had passed out through exhaustion. I wasn't officially infertile although Gilda often made me feel that way. On Saturday nights at the pub she'd have one drink too many and tell everyone I was suffering from "oligospermia". The lads used to back-slap me and give me the "Never mind, you can put it about and she'll never know" routine. But it fell on deaf ears. I couldn't please Gilda anymore and it hurt.

We had our free allocation's worth of treatment on the NHS and when that failed there wasn't the money to spend on more. Eventually we came to accept that we weren't going to be parents. We settled into our old habits and Gilda stopped mentioning the oligospermia. Well, that was until they started doing politically correct stuff at Gilda's work. She was no longer a "sales assistant" but a "sales consultant" and, on weekends, while I fished, she no longer visited her mum or sewed dresses but studied for an NVQ in retail.

Gilda began to change, almost imperceptibly at first, until her boss left to look after her kids and Gilda decided to apply for the manager's position. I was chuffed when she came home with the news that she'd got the job and we celebrated down at the Indian. I thought that maybe the new responsibility would lay the ghost of our childlessness to rest. Well, I guess it did. But not quite the way I expected.

From that day onwards, we spent less time together. Gilda was frequently late home because of problem with the tills, an evening stock delivery or the alarm not setting up. She worked loads of extra hours and before long she was an area manager, packing her Slimfast bars in her briefcase in the morning and striding down the path with the parting line; "I won't be home till late. Don't wait up!"

And I just carried on cleaning windows.

I shuffled around under the umbrella trying to get my body out of the burning sun, took another bite of my cheese and pickle sandwich and gazed out over the river. It was quiet, almost foreboding. Heavy branches of a weeping willow, laden with leaves, drooped in the water on the opposite bank. A lonesome bubble burst on the surface of the water as I savoured my last crust. So far my luck had been abysmal. Even the fish seemed to be asleep, hiding away in the depths and crevices of the riverbed. I snapped open a cold beer and slurped it down in frustration. In the overpowering heat it tasted better than ever. It reminded me of when Gilda and I were young and life was fresh and exciting. When I was going to be more than just a window cleaner and she was going to be a mother.

I guess there hadn't been one definable moment when our relationship turned sour. It was a gradual separation of ways. We hardly slept together anymore, even though Gilda's underwear was becoming more exotic and expensive. It had crossed my mind that the late nights were a cover for an affair but, in the end, I'd put her extravagance down to the extra cash and her yearning for a better life. If we couldn't have a kid then I supposed a luxury car or a fancy kitchen were the next best things. Anyway, that's what I thought. Until I found the condoms. Well, a woman whose husband's six-shooter is firing blanks doesn't need condoms, does she?

Heaving myself up, I brushed the crumbs off my shorts, cupped them in my hands and tossed them into the river. I waded back into the water with my rod and cast out my line again. The sun was even higher now, the skin on my shoulders prickling despite my earlier attempts to lather myself with cream. I wished I'd remembered my hat as a surge of dizziness made the water shimmer and glow with an array of coloured lights.

"Hello, Harry. I thought I'd find you here."

I twisted towards the bank, my vision blurring as my legs remained fixed in the silt like ancient roots. Gilda flashed in and out of focus.

"You look unwell, Harry. Is the heat getting to you?"

"Yes, I think so. I'll come in for another drink in a moment."

"Have you had your lunch yet?"

"Yes, thanks. Your sarnies were great."

"You know, you're not looking good at all."

"It's the heat. I'll be fine."

I wound in my line and splashed water over my face, revelling in the cold droplets cooling my searing skin. As my head began to clear, I saw Gilda still watching sullenly from the embankment. She'd never been able to hide her distaste for my hobby, even in better times.

"About your sandwiches, Harry," said Gilda, a streak of impatience crossing her face. "I think you should know that I poisoned them. In a few minutes, you'll be dead."

Gilda's malevolent words washed over me like an all-consuming wave. I sank to my knees, the water rising to my chest. I knew now the full intensity of Gilda's betrayal. She didn't just want an affair, but a permanent separation. A deadly separation.

"You were always so predictable. I knew you'd eat your sandwiches at midday."

I reeled backwards, my body straining against the current and the impact of Gilda's words.

"You're a useless twat, Harry. I've wasted my life with you. All you think about is your bloody windows and fishing rods," said Gilda, wading through the water until she stood before me.

"You're right. I never had any imagination," I said, looking up at her icy, unforgiving eyes. "I guess I should have stopped cleaning windows."

"Goodbye, Harry."

Gilda reached out and pressed her hands upon my head, using all her weight to push me further into the cold waters. But, as my face slipped under the surface, instinct overcame my lethargy and I seized her leg and began to pull her down with me. Grabbing her waist, I wrenched myself up against her until our roles reversed. Her blue eyes held mine as her mouth bopped in and out of the water, spluttering and gasping like a landed fish.

"Things are a little different now, aren't they?" I said. "It really was the heat, Gilda. There's nothing wrong with me. I'm not dying."

"Harry…I…was…only…joking…"

"No, you weren't," I said, as Gilda's lungs filled with water. "If you hadn't been so wrapped up in yourself, you'd have remembered I don't like prawn sandwiches. I bought some others and threw your's to the birds. They're behind the bushes with some dead sparrows. I thought it was odd…but now I know the truth."

"Harry…"

"Goodbye, Gilda"

I forced her down into the water whilst she mouthed words at me, her eyes bulging wide as her life ebbed away. As her hair trailed behind her in the current, I remembered how she'd looked standing on her head all those years ago when we were young. When we still loved each other.

But we didn't love each other anymore.

When the bubbles stopped rising and her thrashing arms fell limp, I dragged her as far out into the river as I could go, where the current was stronger and faster. I pushed her downstream towards the open sea and watched her sail away, her blonde locks still trailing behind her.

I guess Gilda never recognized the value of good window cleaners. They nearly always do a grand job.

And sometimes, when the grime is too thick, they use plenty of water.

In the Wink of an Eye

Caterpillar tracks. Fresh, impressed deep in the sucking mud. The enemy lurks nearby, somewhere close. You feel them in your bones, taunting you.

A stench of sickly sulphur, fetid corpses and manic fear hangs in the air. *Rat a tat tat, rat a tat tat.* Your heart pounds, trickles of sweat run down your grimy face. Anxiously you glance around, dilated pupils flickering over ravaged trees, burning trucks and smouldering wreckage. You pause a second longer on the decapitated head of Sean Watts. Poor bastard.

You take another look. Fuck. Did he wink at you?

Sinking down into the mire, wet sludge clings onto your combats like curds of brown rancid butter. The heavy backpack weighs you down, pushing you deeper into the sodden earth. Stay alive, stay hidden. *Rat a tat tat, rat a tat tat.* Duty calls, there's no time for sentiment or grief. Remember your training. Block out Sean's face stricken in macabre astonishment.

But you wonder if he knows something that you don't.

Fight, not flight. You crawl across the slime, belly wet, face blackened with stripes like a serpent of death. You find Sergeant Hughes crouched in a shell hole. *Where to now, Sarge?* No reply. You push his shoulder. *Now what, Sarge?* Then you notice the warm stickiness on your fingers, the hands clasping a split stomach, slippery entrails protruding through bloody fingers. You slump back, breath short.

So Sean did know.

An eerie whistle screams overhead, the earth shakes, explodes. Mud rains down like a plague of locusts, consuming you. Pinpricks of rainbow lights appear before your eyes and the sun begins to shine through the wetness. Heat spreads through your limbs and torso.

Ring, ring, ring. You shake your head furiously. *Ring, ring, ring.* It's 8.50 am. Your knees are grubby from the fall. Don't get messy before school, Robbie. Clean up quickly before the teacher sees you. Hurry, before you line up. You struggle to your feet, body aching as a voice calls across the playground. *Robbie, Robbie!* Too late. You're in trouble now.

But it's not the teacher, it's Karen. She runs towards you, arms outstretched, white veil billowing behind, the train of her dress catching on thorny shrubs. A small boy follows, thumb in mouth, clasping a toy rabbit by the foot, the long soft ears stroking the uneven ground. You drop your gun and reach out to greet them, overjoyed. *Karen, Tommo, I'm here!* But Karen runs past, across the pitted clearing and back into the woods. Tommo trails after her, mud squelching through his toes.

And Superman on his pyjamas winks at you.

The ringing fades as you hear the crushing of undergrowth, the tearing of branches, an unmistakable throbbing, pulling engine. *Rat a tat tat, rat a tat tat.* Shouts, screams, rise above the shuddering ground. A grey, hideous monster appears, compressing debris, churning the earth. It strikes fear in you standing defenceless in its deadly shadow. *Rat a tat tat, rat a tat tat.* You turn to run and wonder if God is on your side.

When you awake you hear gentle murmuring and distant echoing voices. You feel warmth, comfort. Safe at last. Maybe God was on your side. Slowly, you open your eyes, blurred shapes move to and fro. You begin to focus on the black silhouette at your side, the white collar, the familiar face.

And then he winks at you.

Hello, mate.

White Lies

William Baxter crosses the marble foyer towards the exit, his sharp steps and abrupt conversation distracting the security guard from his panel of surveillance cameras.

"Tell the lawyers to get the documents drawn up by close of business or they can kiss my ass. Bunch of lazy fuckers."

Baxter senses the interest of the guard as he replaces the phone in his pocket.

"Good morning, Mr Baxter," says the guard, touching his cap.

Baxter gives a cursory nod of recognition, even though he knows the guard indulges the rumour that he murdered his mother. Unfortunately, when you've a reputation as a man who pulls off impossible deals and bankrupts other businesses, malicious gossip is always rife. Baxter's learnt to live with rumours and shrugs them off as inconsequential gossip. As for the rumour he murdered his mother – Baxter grins.

Baxter ignores the fanciful stares of two secretaries and quickens his pace, securing the buttons on his cashmere coat with one hand and stealing a glimpse at his Rolex on the other. He pushes the revolving doors with an impatient thrust and steps out onto the sunlit sidewalk. A limousine pulls up, light ricocheting off its polished silver fender. Baxter has fifteen minutes to travel four blocks to Saviour Investments. Since he made a killing on the stock exchange this morning, he's decided to make them an offer they can't refuse. The driver opens the car door. Baxter strides towards it when a sudden impact throws him off-balance and sends him staggering backwards.

"For fuck's sake!" curses Baxter, straightening up and preparing to give his assailant a lashing of abuse. But there's no suited employee to take the brunt of his anger, only a dishevelled young woman lying on the sidewalk.

"Mr Baxter," says his driver. "Let me deal with it…"

"No, no. It's all right. I'll see to it," says Baxter, waving the driver away.

Baxter inspects the woman, making a quick appraisal of her worn heels, tired skirt and saggy jumper. He's distracted from the spilled contents of her handbag by her skirt which has ridden up exposing the smooth creamy flesh of her legs splayed wide on the dirty concrete. The desire for academic victory over Saviour seems less urgent as Baxter feels the stirrings of unexpected lust.

"I'm sorry, I didn't see you," says the woman.

Tearing his eyes away from the naked skin and hints of flimsy underwear, Baxter notices the dark glasses askew on a youthful face with a surge of disappointment. He distrusts people, particularly women, who wear sunglasses, especially when it's dull and overcast. He wonders what the woman may be hiding: puffy eyes from a sleepless night, a bout of tears or something else? He remembers his mother's cutting asides dispensed from behind her designer glasses, a cigarette poised at her lips. Defence or attack? He's never quite sure.

As Baxter surveys the scene, he spots an unmistakable object on the sidewalk and admonishes himself for not being more observant. He normally notices even the smallest details including the unintentional vocal nuances and facial grimaces which, in the boardroom, have put him one step ahead of the pack. But today he has been too preoccupied with thoughts of subjugation as, not only did he not see the woman, but he did not see her white cane.

"Hello…hello?" says the woman, her voice wavering.

Words stick in Baxter's throat for a moment as the woman briefly tilts her head to one side before turning to scrabble around for the missing cane and the scattered contents of her bag.

"I was in a hurry and didn't see you either," says Baxter, kneeling on the floor. At the same time as Baxter regrets the dirt on his pants, he's aware of an emotion he has not felt for a long time. So long, he was not even sure it still existed.

"I thought you'd left," says the woman, turning back towards him.

"No…I was winded," replies Baxter. He picks up her bag, reaches for her hand and guides it so she can drop her collection of possessions back inside. "I'm fine now. Are you?"

"Yes. I was just disorientated for a moment," says the woman.

Baxter admires the fact she hasn't demonized him or referenced her blindness. He picks up the remaining articles and deposits them alongside the others, a fleeting glimmer of curiosity passing over his face as he absorbs the information they reveal:

Mary Anne Whitmore.

Baxter picks up the cane, places it in Mary Anne's hand and holds her by the other.

"Let me help you up. Ready now? One, two, three!"

Baxter pulls Mary Anne to her feet. He doesn't release her hand but studies her as she steadies herself; she's taller than he expected with long lustrous hair befitting his bedroom pillows, and her unusual looks, if accentuated by the right makeup, would make women jealous and men licentious.

"Thank you," says Mary Anne, pulling her hand out of his grasp.

"I should make up for my clumsiness," says Baxter with deliberation. "Do you like Italian?"

"No need," replies Mary Anne. "It was an accident."

"I won't take no for an answer," says Baxter. "Please accept my offer by way of an apology. If you prefer, we could make it French or Thai."

"I have an appointment."

"Whatever it is, I'm sure it can wait," says Baxter.

"No…it can't," says Mary Anne and turns away, her cane leading the way.

Baxter observes Mary Anne's stilted progress down the sidewalk. He's intrigued by her stubbornness and her blindness, but his fleeting compassion dissolves as she merges with the crowd. As she disappears completely, he wipes the dust from his pants and realizes he's aroused by the idea that she can't see him for who he really is.

* * * * *

"Wanker."

Baxter hears the muted insult as he acknowledges the offer of coffee from the secretary, whose curvaceous breasts press against her blouse revealing the imprint of her lacy bra. She smiles provocatively. But instead of visualizing the blonde beauty sucking his cock, Baxter imagines Mary Anne Whitmore on her knees while he winds his hands through her dark locks and urges her to take him deeper.

Turning back to the board table, his face composed, Baxter stirs his coffee. He sips the bitter sludge and scans the room for the man who slighted him. He concludes it is either the grey-haired executive, whose antagonism is marked on his lined face, or the sharp-suited younger man whose skin has the pallor and sleekness of a ladyboy. Baxter focuses his interest on the older man who returns it with a steady eye. Baxter knows the man is willing him to make an accusation, but Baxter says nothing. He recognises the man would spit on his face, but not on his back. Baxter transfers his interrogation to the younger man who holds his eyes for a moment before flicking an imaginary speck of dust off his sleeve; Baxter has his answer.

"I'm pleased we've come to a settlement," says Baxter, resuming the meeting. He studies his audience, their masks exposed by the unfolding events, and feels no remorse. These are men like him: men who buy and sell; men who take rather than give; men who would win at all costs.

"It's a generous offer," says Saviour's chief executive with resignation. "A buy-out is in the long-term interests of the company, despite the fact that, at present, many of us would prefer to continue as we are."

Baxter nods in understanding. He won't be provoked into unnecessary debate, but he knows acknowledging the discontent will ease potential friction. He doesn't want any obstacles to his agenda.

"This is a successful company and I intend to keep it that way," says Baxter, rising to his feet. "It will only get stronger. In the meantime, I plan to make no immediate structural and management changes."

A collective sigh of relief follows Baxter as he walks towards the door. He turns and relishes his parting line: "Unless, of course, any of you think I'm a wanker."

Baxter shuts the door behind him and gives the secretary a seductive smile. She blushes and touches her hair.

"Fire the ladyboy," says Baxter.

The secretary blushes again and picks up the phone.

* * * * *

Leaning back against the supple leather of his limousine, Baxter studies his spread sheet. He revels in facts and figures, accounts and accountability. He knows statistics can be manipulated and how much can be hidden in rows and columns. Fortunately, Baxter has an aptitude for numbers and analysis, even the most complicated. He can read figures upside down, in red or in black and even in his sleep. But when he wakes he's always converted deficits to surpluses and positives to negatives. And usually with a bonus.

The phrase "accounts and accountability" appeals to Baxter; he'll use it at the next AGM. He removes a pen from his inner breast pocket, which slides between his fingers like the silk of a woman's underwear, and writes the words across the top of the sheet. As the ink caresses the paper, he acknowledges that it was presumptuous to fire the ladyboy before the formalities are finalised. But, then again, Baxter knows Saviour's executives will eagerly step over the carcass before the day is out. His arrogance will only enhance his reputation.

Baxter returns the spread sheet to his briefcase and gazes out of the tinted windows whilst he contemplates whether or not he should have a celebratory glass of champagne with his lunch. As the array of suited employees flow past him like the figures of a Lowry painting, he notices the throng parting and fusing around a woman weaving her way through the crowd. He recognises her as Mary Anne Whitmore.

"Stop," says Baxter.

The driver swerves to the curb. Baxter climbs out and watches Mary Anne seeking out cracks and pitfalls in the sidewalk with her cane. As she approaches, Baxter notices the welfare office in the distance and deduces Mary Anne's appointment was the paperwork that keeps her from falling into total destitution. He speculates if she would have declined his offer of lunch if she could see his wealth and power; the magnet which makes so many men, and women, eager for his company and conversation.

"Mary Anne?"

Mary Anne stops abruptly, startled at the use of her name.

"I assume your appointment has finished. Perhaps now you'd like to accept my invitation?" says Baxter.

"Have you been following me?" says Mary Anne, recognising Baxter's voice.

"I was returning from a meeting and saw you from my taxi. Perhaps it was destiny," says Baxter, "if you believe in such a thing."

"I don't," replies Mary Anne. "And I don't go anywhere with people I don't know."

"I'm not planning on attacking you. I just wanted to… make amends," says Baxter with a salacious grin.

"I'm not sure…"

"Life is full of risks, Mary Anne," interrupts Baxter. "Besides, we're already physically acquainted. It's not as if we're complete strangers."

A pink flush appears on Mary Anne's cheeks at the mention of their first encounter. Baxter steps a little closer, reclaiming Mary Anne's free hand. Her soft skin rekindles his memory of her exposed thighs.

"My name is William. But you can call me Bill. No one else calls me that."

"Let me touch your face," says Mary Anne, as if such intimacy were an everyday occurrence.

Baxter lifts Mary Anne's hand and places it on his cheek. She spreads her fingers and runs them gently over his cheeks, down his nose and traces the outline of his lips. A delicious tingle spreads throughout Baxter, radiating from his scalp, circulating throughout his torso and legs, and trickling into his toes.

"You're a handsome man," says Mary Anne, stepping back.

"Does that matter?" replies Baxter, pining for more of her touch.

"No, but when you're blind very little matters but the truth."

"So, will you dine with me, Mary Anne? Will you trust me?" says Baxter, steering the conversation away from her uncomfortable premise.

"Yes," says Mary Anne after a pause. "I shall trust you."

Baxter helps Mary Anne into his limousine. Her long black hair contrasts with the soft cream leather. Baxter's imagination is captivated by the thought of her hair trailing over his chest, her legs clamped either side of him.

"This isn't a taxi," says Mary Anne, as her hand brushes across the seats.

"I thought you were blind," says Baxter, propelled back into reality by the accuracy of her remark. He removes her sunglasses with a deft swipe.

"Don't touch me," says Mary Anne, cowering back against the passenger door.

Baxter scans Mary Anne's naked face and the secrets behind her glasses.

"There's nothing wrong with your eyes. They're completely normal," says Baxter sinking back into his seat disappointed that Mary Anne has turned out to be another fake.

"I'm almost blind," says Mary Anne, bitterly. "You don't have to look like a freak to be blind. Very soon I will never see the light of day. Is that good enough for you?"

There's a pause as Baxter takes in the news. "No, not really," says Baxter, begrudgingly. "How much can you see?"

"Not much. And what I have is failing rapidly."

"Is there no cure?"

"There are new procedures being developed and trialled all the time. But I'm not a priority. I'm trying to develop my other senses. Learn by association."

Mary Anne strokes the smooth leather of the seats again. Baxter imagines her hands running over him with the same lingering touch.

"Why did you lie to me?" says Mary Anne.

Baxter sees his driver's eyes flick away from the road ahead to look at him in the rear view mirror. Baxter muses over his answer before replying.

"I'm a wealthy and influential man, Mary Anne."

"I see," says Mary Anne, contemplating. "So you wanted to pick me up but didn't want any ties."

"No, you don't see…"

"I think I do…"

"I thought you might be different."

"You mean easier to throw off? Look, why don't you just drop me off here."

"Pull over," says Baxter, losing patience.

The driver pulls sharply to the kerb. Mary Anne fumbles with the door handle.

"I didn't mean what you think," says Baxter reaching across her to let her out. As he does so, her hair brushes his face.

"Your hair… and eyes are extraordinary," says Baxter as Mary Anne makes to leave.

Mary Anne turns to face Baxter again and stares at him. Baxter has no idea what she sees or thinks. Not even when she touches the contours of his face again, her fingers running down his neck onto the collar of his shirt and the fine weave of his suit.

"I like Italian," says Mary Anne.

Mary Anne kneels before Baxter, her dark locks tumbling around her shoulders and brushing against his thighs. He runs his hands through her hair, winds tendrils around his fingers, and clasps her head as he pushes deeper. Baxter knows he is only a shadow in the blurred images of her failing eyesight and it strips away his lies. As Mary Anne's hands flit across his buttocks and her mouth meets his demands, his relief is greater than he could ever have imagined.

* * * * *

Baxter straightens his bow tie and grins at his reflection in the mirror. Tonight is the opening of his latest project: The Baxter Charitable Institute for Ophthalmic Research. In eighteen months Baxter's life has changed completely, as it has for Mary Anne whose sight he has restored with his money and his influence. Baxter's still a major player but, with Mary Anne at his side and in his bed, he no longer dreams of spread sheets or wakes to the sound of a persistent alarm. He delights too that his staff no longer gossip about his mother or call him Satan behind his back. Baxter slaps on his aftershave, grins at himself again and imagines the horns on his head receding. His redemption is almost complete.

"Are you ready yet, Mary Anne?" says Baxter.

"Almost," replies Mary Anne, sweeping into the dressing room wearing a voluptuous gown.

"You look stunning," says Baxter. "I'm lucky you came into my life." Baxter withdraws a necklace from a box and fastens it around Mary Anne's neck.

"Perfect," says Baxter.

* * * * *

Mary Anne studies her eyes in the mirror; they're the colour of rich, dark chocolate with pupils as black as the Devil's. Baxter adores them, and now she does too. The eyes she once cursed have opened up a whole new world for her, a world far more grandiose than the one in which she was born. She steps back and inspects her image, admiring her coiffured hair, sumptuous dress and bejewelled necklace. As she empties the contents of her handbag onto the washstand, searching for her favourite lipstick to complete her transformation, her designer sunglasses slip out and rattle into the sink bowl. She retrieves them, puts them on and examines herself in the mirror once more. Even with the sunglasses, she's totally unrecognisable as the blind woman who walked the streets in worn heels and tired clothes. Baxter's love, and money, have changed her forever.

And in the mirror her horns begin to grow.

The Journey

My hands grip the gate, the cold frame slides open like a mortuary drawer. I slip through, exhaling. It snaps back into place like the sharp recoil of a gun.

A path lies before me, a stretch of pebbled stones giving way to sodden grass and soil. Branches of tall trees hang heavy, trailing like the tresses of a lover's hair. A grey mist meanders, its cold, clammy fingers caressing me until my clothes cling like a second skin.

Mud squelches around my feet, sealing my presence. Sharp thorns and sneering faces taunt me from the dark recesses of the forest. But there is no other path, so I push my hands deep into my pockets, taking comfort in the smooth metal my fingers encounter.

My feet drag and my limbs ache as the path inclines. Sweat trickles down my face. I glance back, my body tingling as the track appears to close behind me. Yet I cannot falter, it's the day I've waited for. The day of reckoning. I shiver and the silence hums like a mother's whisper, cajoling me onwards.

I see him waiting on the crest of the hill, a shadow in the twilight. I clench my fist; feel the imprint on my hand.

He stretches out his hand towards me. I draw out mine.

We are face to face for the first time.

And, as a soft light rises, I place the rosary in his scarred palm.

Sweet and Salty

Fantasia

For decades it had remained a secret, the truth distorted as an urban myth by the claims of wild-eyed fanatics but on December 15th 2031, exactly sixty-five years after his death, Walt Disney opened his eyes.

"How's my Pooh?" he croaked.

I'd anticipated curiosity about his defrosting, the replacement lung and the removal of his cancer cells - but I hadn't expected a fascination with his bowel movements. I consulted the clip chart at the bottom of the bed.

"Your poo is as expected Mr Disney: a little bit soft but not unwholesome for someone who's just come out of suspension and undergone extensive surgery."

"Not poo, you imbecile. Pooh!"

Nurse Erin shrugged and pulled a face suggesting Disney was probably still confused from the medication or, very possibly, just plain bonkers. I opened my Dianote and started to scan post operational symptoms affecting the brain.

"What are you doing?" he croaked louder.

"I'm consulting."

"Consulting with whom?" he replied with an air of distain.

"Consulting the Brainbank." I held up my pocket-sized Dianote. "It's a central medical information resource. It helps me with diagnostics but I can also use it for booking surgery dates and ordering replacement organs."

"Humph," Disney snorted, unimpressed. "I suppose you grow organs from a petri dish."

"Actually, we do," I replied, a hint of smugness creeping into my voice. Disney had only been awake a few seconds and he was already living up to his biographical blurb of being extremely difficult to please. "Originally, we used animal or donated human organs as replacements but then a breakthrough allowed us to grow just about any organ apart from the brain."

Disney snorted again but less so.

"So people still snuff it then?"

"Snuff it?"

"Die," said Disney, impatiently. "Haven't you heard that expression before?"

"Yes, they still die," I replied, trying to ignore Disney's jibe but becoming increasingly irritated. "But the quality of life is much improved. People are fitter and healthier in old age. When they "snuff it" it's because the brain has completed its natural life cycle."

"Hmm," Disney murmured, pulling himself upright.

"Take it easy now, Mr Disney," I said, as Erin adjusted the headrest and plumped the pillows. "Your muscles are still weak."

"What else can that gadget discover?" said Disney, gesturing at my Dianote.

"Pretty much anything."

"So what about my Pooh?"

"As I said, your poo is…"

"Not poo!" he yelled. "Pooh! P. O. O. H."

"Oh, Winnie the Pooh," I exclaimed, as Erin burst out giggling.

"Well of course it's Winnie the Pooh! Do you think I'm some kind of freak?" snapped Disney with a look that now said he thought I was the freak. "So, did I win the Oscar for Winnie in 1967?"

I consulted the Dianote again, trying to suppress my laughter. It was a huge relief I didn't have to transfer Disney to psychotherapy. As the first person to successfully come out of cryogenic suspension, his rehabilitation would be the subject of much medical interest and, no doubt, the peak of my career. But it would all be in jeopardy if Disney was mentally unstable. As it was, he might be peculiar but his mind seemed reasonably intact.

"So did it win?" said Disney impatiently.

"I'm afraid not. However…"

"I don't believe it!" exploded Disney, throwing of his sheets and trying to grab my Dianote.

"Try and keep calm," I replied, leaping back and holding the Dianote out of his reach. "If you get too upset you'll go into cardiac arrest."

"What the hell were those idiots at the Academy doing?" ranted Disney. Winnie the Pooh and the Blustery Day was genius, sheer genius."

"What I was about to say, Mr Disney, was - it won in 1969. Apparently, your death delayed production."

"Ahh,"sighed Disney, flopping back into his pillow with a broad grin. "That is good news."

Disney raised his hand to check if his moustache was still in place and, discovering it was, stroked it with gentle contemplation. Eventually he turned his attention to the room, his eyes surveying it like a snake about to strike. It was clear that Disney's brain was still performing well and that his mental abilities might even surpass all of my predictions. My initial frustrations started to turn to excitement as I realised it was possible my research into brain function might develop faster than I'd anticipated.

"What year is it?" said Disney, focussing his attention on me again.

"2031."

"I'm a hundred and thirty years old?" said Disney, his mouth agape like a feeding fish.

"Yes, and today is the sixty-fifth anniversary of your suspension."

"Incredible! And to think I have almost seventy years of films to catch up on," said Disney, shaking his head from side to side in disbelief.

"And a few other things too," I smiled.

"Now, where's the television in here?" said Disney, looking around the room again. "I can't be without a television!" Disney's voice faltered for this first time. "You do still have television?"

"Yes, of course," I replied, walking across the room and picking up the controller off the side table and switching it on so the image of Marilyn Monroe on the side wall faded away to be replaced by the central menu of the latest visualisation screen.

"I had no idea there was anything there!" said Disney. "Except poor Marilyn. Wonderful actress but completely barking mad."

"Don't worry - television is still a huge form of entertainment," I laughed and concluded that Disney's rehabilitation might be a lot less painful than I'd originally thought. Not only would I be on the threshold of new medical research but I'd also have access to my own living history book.

"And my films? Do people still watch my films?"

"Yes indeed, Mr Disney. Everyone still loves your films…and Winnie the Pooh of course. They're all classics."

"Excellent, excellent. Now when do I start?" Disney clapped his hands together playfully. "I want to see what's been happening in the world!"

"It's all here," I said, putting down the controller and taking a microstore from its storage case. "Sixty years of films, news reports, documentaries, political speeches. Everything to bring you up to date."

"All that is on this?" he replied, taking the microstore and holding it between his thumb and index finger. "It's no bigger than my fingernail!"

"They're two of them actually," I grinned. "Sixty-five years is a long time."

"Incredible, incredible," said Disney, turning the microstore over and over in amazement.

"Many of the changes that have happened, especially this century, have been out of absolute necessity," I replied. "We've had to find solutions to problems like climate change that sixty years ago you may never have imagined."

"Hmm," muttered Disney, screwing his eyes up as if trying to picture scenes on film. "Climate change? Now there's something I hadn't anticipated. Are we in the midst of an ice age?"

"No, almost the opposite. The atmosphere has warmed up and it's making the weather patterns erratic."

"But the weather has always been erratic," exclaimed Disney.

"But not quite like it is now."

"You've just become too soft with all your fancy gadgets. You need to toughen up!" grunted Disney. "Surely, it can't be that bad?"

"You really want to know?"

"But of course!" replied Disney, banging his fists down on his starched white sheets. "I'm not an imbecile!"

Reluctantly, I pressed a button on the controller and the window blind covering the far wall slid up into the ceiling.

"Impressive," said Disney, sarcastically.

"The window or the weather?"

"The window, obviously, you idiot," yelled Disney. "I can't see anything beyond some heavy rain lashing on the window. It's obviously the middle of the night!"

"It's ten o'clock in the morning."

"Oh."

Disney fell silent, his eyes following droplets of water running down the window and pooling on the bottom of the frame. After a few minutes I pressed the button on the controller again and the blind dropped down blocking out what little there was to see. I flicked the visualization screen onto the climate channel. Disney watched in silence as the reporter gave a run down on the latest weather reports, and images of towns submerged by the sea or abandoned through drought and decimation flickered across the screen.

"It seems a lot has happened since I left," said Disney sullenly, placing the microstore carefully on his bedside table.

"It takes thirty years for the carbon emissions that cause global warming to reach their full effect," I explained, switching off the visualization screen. "It could be years before the weather stabilizes. Or it may never stabilize. We just don't know what lies ahead."

"Maybe…maybe…I should start simply with tea and a newspaper?" said Disney.

Perhaps now was not a good time to tell him about some of the other things that had happened. But then Disney was no fool. He certainly wasn't the sort of man you could deceive for very long.

"Unfortunately, they're no newspapers anymore, Mr Disney," I replied gently. "Wood is a protected source now. And you need a licence to print books."

"No newspapers? Licences for books? I can't believe it! What sort of world have I woken up to?" blurted Disney in despair, closing his eyes and massaging his forehead.

"Some good things have happened too," I countered, searching for the right words to soothe his obvious disappointment. "Everyone loved The Jungle Book and the song The Bare Necessities was nominated for an Oscar…"

"And rightly so," interrupted Disney, looking haughty again. "So it won?"

"Um…no," I replied, quickly realising I'd made a very poor error of judgement.

"Did it win anything then?"

"Um…no."

"Are you a doctor or a comedian?" yelled Disney, the blood vessels on his neck bulging and his words echoing around the room. "I wake up after sixty-five years and you tell me that not only did The Jungle Book not win any Oscars but the world is in crisis and I can't even read a newspaper! What's next? I can't wipe my backside?"

"Ah…well," I mumbled, looking at Erin for support. "Did you have hand dryers back in the Sixties?"

"Of course we did. I'm not a dinosaur!" yelled Disney back at me even more furiously. "And before you ask – yes, we did have fire!"

"I know it's difficult, Mr Disney," I replied, edging closer to his intravenous drip. "But you really must try and stay calm or I'll have to sedate you. I can't risk any complications at this early stage."

Sedating Disney was become a very attractive proposition. I gestured discreetly to Erin to move closer, ready to hold him down by force if necessary.

"Don't you dare knock me out," shouted Disney, as if he could read my thoughts. "I've been dead for sixty-five years and now I want to be alive!"

"Well - be a good patient then!" I retorted, finally losing my patience.

We stared at each other like two resolute gladiators, each of us determined not to be manipulated by the other. Eventually, Disney broke the silence.

"So how exactly do I dry my arse?"

* * * * *

"This is amazing - a chair with multidirectional sensors and kinetic energy – who'd have thought of it!" said Walt, as I accompanied him to the 1950s style cinema his family had recreated for him in the basement. "But these chairs are very solitary companions. I don't mind taking a leak by myself but being alone all the time? It doesn't stir the creative juices."

"But the Comfortchair gives far greater freedom and manoeuvrability."

"I still prefer being pushed."

"I'm beginning to think you're lazy, not that you're tired, Walt."

"Tell that to my bank manager and I think he'll dispute it," said Walt, adjusting his cravat and sticking his nose pompously in the air.

I laughed. Over the past few weeks I'd become increasingly fond of Walt and his sharp tongue. He was stubborn, temperamental and terribly arrogant yet there was something fascinating about him. He had wonderful stories to tell about his life and generation of course - yet there was something else about him too. Something I couldn't quite define.

"What films am I watching today, Corey?" said Disney eagerly, rubbing his hands together as if about to consume some luxurious feast.

"I've picked out some that I thought would be of interest to you from a cinematographer's point of view."

"Now that's more like it, said Disney his eyes shining brightly. "How exciting! That film I watched yesterday with its apocalyptic scenario was so depressing I wanted to bury myself in my popcorn."

I laughed again. Walt was always so melodramatic. I'd got used to his fiery temper and ebullient displays of emotion and instead of being upset or embarrassed as I was at first, now I found it hugely entertaining.

"Walt, I was trying to educate you about the way recent films have reflected what's been happening in the world," I replied. "Not all of life is a cartoon."

"Yes, yes, Corey," said Walt, impatiently. "But all those depressing films are not good for the soul. People need love and laughter more than they need tragedy and tears. They need uplifting stories that inspire. Not all that end of the world, eaten alive by monsters stuff," said Walt, pulling a disgusted face. "Aliens bursting out of people's stomachs and crawling up noses? Ugh! It quite puts me off my tea."

I laughed again and manoeuvred Walt alongside a row of plush red velvet seats.

"Is it true what they say," said Walt, switching to his serious mode as I adjusted the angle of his chair, "that New York and London are flooding?"

"I'm afraid so. Tokyo and Mumbai too. And they will continue to flood as coastal regions are more at risk. All we can do now is limit the damage; use new technologies to curb carbon emissions, build defences, repair what we can."

"But why didn't people believe the scientists?" said Walt.

"Who knows, Walt? Ignorance, greed, stupidity?"

"Hmm," murmured Disney, lost in his own thoughts.

"I'll be back during the day to check on you." I said, handing Walt his Ablenote, a standardized version of my

Dianote. "Don't forget you can contact Erin for anything you need."

I walked back to the door as the lights dimmed and a red neon exit light glowed in the dark.

"Oh, I've ordered you some more popcorn," I called back up the aisle.

"But why, Corey, why? That's what I can't understand," called Walt in return.

"I thought you liked it."

"No, not popcorn," sighed Walt. "I mean why didn't people listen to the scientists?"

"I'm a doctor, Walt. I don't know," I replied. "My purpose is to cure, not to reason."

I closed the door and wondered if Walt, the fantasist, would ever come to terms with reality.

* * * * *

It was late afternoon when I returned to the cinema. I'd expected to hear sound effects and voices blasting out with the digital clarity which had, at first, totally overwhelmed Walt. But now, as I opened the door, all was quiet.

"Walt?"

There was no reply. I quickly checked the tracker on my Ablewatch. Walt hadn't moved for the last two hours. I peered into the darkness.

"Walt?"

It was then I heard soft, muffled sobbing.

"Dim lights please."

The lights flicked on and I saw Walt slouched in his Comfortchair, head in hands, weeping. I walked down the aisle and sat next to him in one of the velvet seats.

"What's the matter?"

"Nothing," sobbed Walt through his fingers.

I pulled one of his hands away from his face and held it firmly.

"Walt, when people cry there is always a reason."

"No, no. I'm fine. Honestly."

"Was it the film? Was it Star Wars?" I said, worried that my choice of films had upset Walt again. "I know all that Death Star business is depressing in a way but those special effects were awesome in their day."

"No, no, it's not Star Wars," said Walt, still snuffling. "It's a marvellous film. I love those light sabres. It's a perfect story where good triumphs over evil. Perfect. Apart from the wooden looking actor of course. Pinocchio could have done a better job."

"Then what is it? What's the matter?" I asked, not knowing whether to laugh or cry.

"It's Toy Story," said Walt, bursting into tears again.

"But Toy Story is brilliant! When I was a child, I watched it over and over again; I even had a Buzz Lightyear."

"But that's it you see," wept Walt. "It is brilliant. Utterly brilliant. And it's made by my company!"

"You're a vain old goat," I chuckled.

"But Corey, I never dreamt entertainment, films, animation would be so amazing," hiccupped Walt.

"Toy Story was just the beginning. You haven't seen Avatar yet. It was one of the first significant films in 3D."

"Three dimensions? But I was experimenting with that years ago. It's nothing new."

"Yes, but now it works properly, Walt. And it doesn't stop there. They can make animations so realistic sometimes it's hard to distinguish them from traditional films with actors."

"Unbelievable!"

"And the latest development is that you can wear a headset which visually transports you inside a film where everything around you is in 3D."

"How do you mean?" said Disney with a frown.

"Imagine being able to stand alongside Darth Vader or Mickey Mouse or even an alien so that you could almost reach out and touch them."

I pressed a button on the armrest of the nearest velvet chair and the back of the seat in front popped open. I removed a Cinenote and handed it to Walt.

"Do you want to try?" I said.

"It looks like a tiara," said Walt, grimacing. "I can't wear that. I'll look like Cinderella."

"Walt, there's absolutely no chance you'll look like Cinderella. You're a hundred and thirty year old man with a moustache."

"Point taken," said Walt. "I'll just look like a jerk then."

Walt put the Cinenote on his head and glared defiantly at me. The multi-sensory nodules glittered like tinsel on a Christmas tree.

"You look like a jerk," I said.

"I knew it," said Walt dramatically. "Whoever designed this has appalling taste."

"I designed it."

"You did?" gawped Walt.

"Yes."

"That proves I'm right then," said Walt. "Look at that shirt you're wearing."

I glanced down towards my orange shirt with the pink trim just visible beneath my doctor's coat.

"I thought it was nice," I said trying not to sound too wounded.

"Think again," said Walt. "Stick to science, Corey. Trust me - fashion isn't your strong point."

"Well, as a doctor and scientist," I said defensively. "I'm more concerned with function rather than design. The Cinenote was an indirect result of my exploration into brain activity. I didn't actually finalise the appearance. Now do you want to try it or do you want to sit there looking like a fairy?"

"Yes, yes. Of course I want to try it," grinned Walt.

"Good," I grinned in return. Now, I'll select a film and you can try it out. Something you're familiar with so you're not too shocked by any of the action. How about a remake of Fantasia?"

"Excellent," said Walt.

I selected Fantasia from the menu on the control panel, the lights dimmed again and the nodules on the Cinenote lit up in an array of colours. Walt's face began to convulse into all sorts of weird and wonderful expressions, his arms gripping the sides of his Comfortchair like a vice as he was transported into his own cinematic world. After a few minutes Walt's feet began to move up and down like a sleeping dog dreaming of chasing rabbits. I checked Walt's pulse on my Ablewatch and decided to turn the Cinenote off. Too much excitement would not be good for his blood pressure.

"Noooooooooooooooo," yelled Walt, as the lights went up. I was just about to fly with Mickey!"

"One small step at a time, Walt," I replied. "I don't want you overdoing it."

"You're a genius!" cried Walt, shaking his head in awe. "I was actually inside a film. I danced with Mickey. I ran with him – I could even smell him! He smelt…like…like…a mouse."

I chuckled and waited for Walt to absorb everything he'd learnt.

"All these things I've missed," said Walt eventually. "So many possibilities."

"You'll soon catch up," I said, patting his back.

"Maybe," said Disney, deep in thought.

"Corey?"

"Yes?"

"Did Disney Productions make Avatar?"

"No."

"Blast," said Walt, vehemently. "Now I shall have to create something better. And you're going to help me!"

I laughed out loud whilst Walt set his Comfortchair in motion and zoomed off towards the exit.

"Come on, Corey. I've got work to do!"

"You know, Walt, for a man who's just come back from the dead you can be very demanding."

"Just call me Jesus," said Walt, turning his head and winking.

* * * * *

Walt began to write. In the mornings he watched films and in the afternoons he wrote on paper I'd sourced from an exclusive retailer. His evenings alternated between periods of research and entertaining the handful of relatives who knew of his existence. In between all this activity Walt and I would enjoy each other's company, often talking well into the night on almost any subject that sparked his curiosity. It was a surprisingly long time though before he raised the matter of how he was brought back to life.

"Am I the only one?" he said one evening as we sipped malt whiskey and leant over the balcony of his room, watching the trickle of patients and staff walking in the grounds.

"At this moment in time? Yes. There have been others, of course, but no one who has survived more than a few weeks. But everything we learnt from them helped us to bring you back to life."

"That's an eerie thought," replied Walt, swirling his malt slowly around his glass.

"I guess so – but the others were brain dead and knew nothing about it. Besides, science has been experimenting with the dead for centuries."

"You know, I never really thought I would live again, Corey," said Walt, thoughtfully. "It was a fantasy I signed up to when I knew I was a goner. I just wasn't ready to die – there were so many more things I wanted to do."

"Even with all the study and research I've done your survival is still utterly flabbergasting," I replied, refilling our glasses. "It may never happen again. Cryogenics is illegal now. There were too many charlatans preying on vulnerable people; too many scientific problems; too much expense and far too many ethical dilemmas."

"So why carry on experimenting? Why am I here?"

"Cryogenics is now about extending life before death. Preserving the body and mind in a healthy state so we can look to explore space, touch the boundaries of our existence."

"And to think all I dreamt of was cartoons and here's you wanting to travel to the edges of the universe."

"With the world in crisis, what better time to explore? Imagine if we were to find new resources, new life elsewhere. It might help."

"But what if you met an alien?"

"Between you and me, Walt. I think it's unlikely," I laughed. "Although I'm not ruling it out. But you can't look to the future with fear, only with hope."

"Hmm…you're right," said Walt, with a pensive expression in his eyes. "People need hope."

* * * * *

So the weeks turned to months and although Walt grew stronger he made no attempt to leave the Institute. He continued to write and my research began to intensify. His compliance with the numerous tests on his mental faculties and physical abilities was easier than I expected. In return, he'd request the company of my family and over tea he would quiz us about our lives: our daily routines, the challenges we faced, our beliefs and hopes for the future. My children were flattered by his interest in them but were far more excited by his extraordinary tales which he often acted out by swashbuckling with crutches, flapping sheets and racing around in his Comfortchair mimicking lasers, tornados and spaceships or whatever strange and wondrous concept entered his fertile imagination. It was hard to believe that Walt, a man who was so very much alive, had ever been dead.

As time passed, I noticed that Walt's labours at his desk became more frantic. Sometimes I caught glimpses of drawings and cartoons as he shuffled his papers or as they lay in crumpled balls around his wastepaper bin. Each time I would remind him not to be so frivolous with his paper until eventually he began smoothing it out and putting it back in his drawer to recycle. Then one evening, after a particularly long bout of writing, I found him sleeping peacefully, his hands clasped over a bulky file lying on his chest.

"Corey?" said Walt.

"I thought you were asleep," I said, turning back from the door.

"No, just thinking," he squinted.

"Nothing too serious I hope."

"I've been thinking it's time I should leave."

I had known that one day Walt would want to return to the outside world. His existence, shrouded in secrecy, meant that he would have to take on a new identity but he would always be a free man, permitted to do as he pleased. But now that day had actually arrived I felt a deep sadness; Walt had become not only my patient, but my friend and confidant.

"You're well enough now, Walt," I said, keeping my voice level. "I can make the arrangements whenever you wish."

"I don't mean that 'leave', I mean the other one."

"I don't understand."

"It's time for me to go back to sleep."

"Sleep?" I felt a lump rising in my throat as I realised what Walt really meant. "You can't be serious. You can't do it. Why would you put yourself through all this just to be suspended again?"

"I suppose this is not my time or place, Corey. I'm not sure if I actually have one anymore. I've loved every minute of this life though. Seeing how the world has changed, all your wonderful inventions and cures. It's been more than any man could dream of."

"We've messed up," I choked. "That's why isn't it? We've messed up our world."

"Every generation messes up in some way, Corey. Look what my generation did – we started two catastrophic world wars. But it's what we learn from it that shapes our future."

"You're afraid for our future –is that it? Is that why you don't want to be here?"

"No, I'm not afraid, Corey. In fact, I want to see that future because I see plenty of things that are good in this world: how technology is saving the rainforests, feeding the starving, combating climate change. I want to see what happens next. I want to see if you make it to the stars."

"You want to live in the future again? That's lunacy, Walt! At least in this generation you still have an immediate connection to the past. But in another hundred years, two hundred years…"

"We all make choices, Corey. And mine is to live again."

I looked towards the window so that Walt would not see the tears in my eyes; the sun was setting, red and crimson stripes sinking beneath the horizon.

"Is there anything, anything at all, I can say that will change your mind?" I said.

"I doubt it, My Boy," replied Walt.

I took a last look at the sunset and closed the blind.

* * * * *

Walt lay in his chamber, dressed in a pristine white gown. There would be no pain of dying like before. He would simply fall asleep, suspended in time by the science which I had helped to develop. Science which I knew now, more than ever, meant he would live again to see the future of the human race. He would discover what I could only dream of. He would learn if we conquered the elements and vanquished our fears, whether we sourced from the stars and touched the edges of the universe.

"Are you sure?" I said.

"I'm sure."

"What date shall I set?"

"Let's leave it to fate."

I set the dial to "random" knowing there was very little chance we would meet again.

"Take this, My Boy," said Walt, handing me the file that contained his writing and drawings. "Give it to my family. Tell them it's to be made into a film. And if I wake up in a hundred years and find it hasn't, there will be hell to pay."

"Don't I know it," I said, my smile tinged with sadness.

I closed the glass lid on his chamber, my heart thudding loud as Walt prepared to go into the unknown once more.

"Goodbye," mouthed Walt.

"Goodbye," I replied.

I pressed the activation button as Walt closed his eyes. And, as he took his last breath, my tears fell on the buff cover of the file like rain upon golden sand.

* * * * *

Walt's film won every award. The story of a bear and his friends who saved a dying world became the biggest box office success of all time. People queued in the streets, in cities and towns, in the East and in the West, all over the world to see Winnie the Pooh and the Medicine Man. The film was a tale of almost impossible deeds in which a man, his bear and their friends Buzz, Mickey and Donald took on the might of the satanic Emperor Weatherman, a malevolent ruler who controlled the elements with a rod sculptured from ore at the centre of the universe. Walt transported people inside the film so that they could share Pooh's incredible adventures. So they could run, fly, cry, laugh and fight alongside Pooh. So they could experience all that Pooh did and in doing so people realised that using all their knowledge they could save the earth from the clutches of the evil Weatherman, break the rod of ore and make their world safe once more.

And so, because of Walt's film, people began to truly believe they could change the world. They finally understood that every man, woman and child and every ruler, nation and continent must work together so their children might inherit the future. Pooh and his friends gave people hope that nothing and no one is beyond redemption. Pooh made people understand that while there is only one future, there will always be many paths on its unending journey.

I am a medicine man. I explore new ways to heal the sick and I cure with the aid of technology, vaccines and antibiotics. But there are those whose cures are far greater. We are lucky if we meet them. I may never see my friend Walt again but I smile, every day, knowing we are always together on film.

Acknowledgements

This collection of stories represents much of my writing journey and exploration into the world of creative writing. I am indebted to The View From Here literary magazine and the BBC for giving me the opportunity to develop my novice writing skills. I am even more indebted to the author, Gary Davison, and to my friend, Elizabeth Axford, who have between them acted as beta-readers for almost all of my fictional work and published articles, provided endless encouragement and spurred me on to the completion of my forthcoming novel, The Changing Room. Without Elizabeth and Gary, my journey would have been so much harder. I have also to thank Eve Merrier who edited White Lies and proofread A Modern Life and who has provided me with a professional and patient sounding-board in the lead-up to publication. My thanks also go to my good friend, Jean Bailey, for her emotional support and to all my other numerous friends, too many to mention, who have indulged my literary musings without slashing their wrists in my presence. Finally, I must thank my husband, my children, my chickens, my cats, the man who delivers my groceries and, most importantly, the many people who have visited my blog The Witty Ways of a Wayward Wife over the years and who have inspired me to keep writing - my thanks to you all - and my apologies for the continued jokes in poor taste.

Author Biography

Jane Turley doesn't take herself too seriously and believes laughter is the best medicine for life's ills. She attributes her sense of humour to her childhood spent gazing out of a Silver Cross pram in the seaside resort of Weston-super-Mare. Her excessive exposure to salty air and seagull poop left Jane with an unfortunate desire to inflict her dubious wit on everyone, including passing strangers, scarecrows and stray dogs. Unsurprisingly, sometimes people think she's odd.

Jane now lives in a village in central England where folks are very kind and give her sympathetic looks when she talks too much.